Sarah *Smile*

Halos & Horns: Book Two

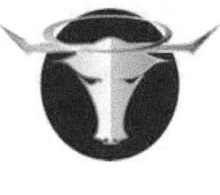

BY
LORI LEGER

ISBN-10: 0-9857192-8-1
ISBN-13: 978-0-9857192-8-9

CAJUNFLAIR
PUBLISHING

P.O. Box 641
Kinder, LA. 70648
www.CajunflairPublishing.com
http://www.facebook.com/CajunflairPublishing

DEDICATION

I'm dedicating this book to all my peeps at Dr. James Maze's Radiation Oncology Clinic at Lake Charles Memorial Hospital in Lake Charles, Louisiana. Dr. Maze and his crew were all so friendly and professional during the time I had my treatments there (2009) They made a difficult situation much easier to handle. You, along with Dr. William Moss, comprise a great team and are much appreciated for all you've done as I creep up on the 5th anniversary of being 'cancer free'.

ACKNOWLEDGMENTS

To my wonderful husband, Michael. You will always be my hero. And to our grandchildren…from eighteen to under a year…you are all adored!

Special thanks to Kim Killion of The Killion Group for the fabulous cover design, yet again.
www.thekilliongroupinc.com

Alice Clary for her editing skills

Joan Granger of Simple Memories Photography In Welsh, LA for the fabulous photo of the author.
www.simplememories.org/index.htm

Once again, to the two tiny book stores with big hearts who carried my books long before anyone else did:

Sean and James Gayle of **Patti's Book Nook** in My old home-town of Gueydan, La.
www.pattisbooknook.com
and
Christy Lepretre of **Books-n-Java** in Jennings, La.
www.booksnjava.com

I'd like to acknowledge my niece and nephew, Sarah and Mitchell Hebert, who lost their father to cancer when they were still kids. I know that their dad, my brother, Gordon, would be proud of both of them, and he would absolutely adore his four beautiful grandchildren. I want to stress that although I named two characters in this and the previous book after them, *in no way* do the character's lives parallel the real Mitch and Sarah's, and nor are they meant to.

JAMAICAN SLANG

She grow mi – She raised me

Jesum Piece. - That's a piece of work! He or She is something.

Kyaan - (Can't)

Yu lub har kyaan done. - Your love for her cannot be undone. (You love her a lot)

Rahtid - (Damn!)

Gweh – go away

Sidung – sit down

Sum'ady - somebody

Fass-Nosey

Dweet-Do it

See you inna di lights.- See you tomorrow.

Mi naa jesta. - I'm not joking or I'm serious.

Si 'ow yu stay? - (Do you see how you are?)

Stoosh – rich

Mi live inna stoosh place. -(I live in a rich place.)

Nuh su-su pon mi bak.- (Don't gossip behind my back)

Na mek mi vex, mon! - (Don't make me mad, man)

"Mi huk yup wid har? - You want me to introduce you to her? Want me to hook you up with her?

U.S. MARINE TERMINOLOGY

Check fire – order to stop firing due to a mistarget or error.

Blooper OR Thump Gun - grenade launcher

Back on the block – behaving like a civilian

AHA – Ammunition Holding Area (where ammo is stored).

Broke Dick – Marine off duty for medical reasons

Call out OR Drop a dime– issue a challenge with incriminating evidence

Civ div – return to civilian life

C & S – Clean and sober

D & D – drunk and disorderly

DI – Drill Instructor

EAS – end of active service or discharge

GI shower – bathing with wipes or limited water

Good to go – satisfactory

Grab-ass – horse play

HE – high explosives

Head – bathroom

Inkstick – pen

Nuts to butts – standing in line extremely close

O-dark thirty – very early hours before dawn

OOB – Out of Bounds

OM – Oscar Mike – On the move

Pucker factor – high level of anxiety in stressful situations

Rack or Sack – bed

Sandbox – desert

Scullery – where dishes are washed

Secure – put away or lock up as in secure the area

Secret squirrel – intelligence personnel or activities

Shit-brick – useless or ignorant person

Snot locker – nose

SSDD – same shit different day

Chapter 1

Sarah Richard would have known that sinfully-sexy profile anywhere. Two months with no sign of Tanner Collins lessened neither his good looks, nor her attraction to him—somewhat intense for your average, friendly crush. Then again, a person would be hard-pressed to describe Tanner in any way other than leaps and bounds *above* average.

His bronzed arm looped the waist of his dinner guest, a glamorously gorgeous, model-thin type. Sarah had no problem imagining the leggy redhead leaving a Victoria's Secret photo shoot to lunch with the handsome Dr. Collins.

His gaze found hers immediately, acknowledging her with a slight nod and the barest hint of a smile in his brilliantly blue eyes. Her heart skittered for several seconds before resuming its normal rhythm.

A voice, sharp with disapproval, resounded from the chair across from her to jolt her from her drooling.

"Hmph, even I thought Tanner had better taste than that."

Sarah turned to her lunch partner, Annie LeBlanc. "Do you know her?" Annie's derisive snort told her she did, but her further comments filled in the blanks.

"Her name's Yvette. She used to be married to Dr. Daniels, an orthopedic surgeon from Lafayette General. We called him 'Dan the Man' in nursing school. He gave the best lectures on anatomy and was always bragging about his beautiful wife, and saying how lucky he was to have her. Then he got cancer. While he was near death in the hospital, a nurse caught her screwing around with some musician, in a vacant room of the same wing. Yvette had the nerve to act put out at the interruption. Told the nurse to get the hell out and shut the door."

Sarah watched as the couple took their seats at their own table. "I'd hate to form an opinion on a rumor," she said.

"It's no rumor. My sister is the one who caught her. Some of the other personnel snapped some incriminating shots and video of them."

"Did anyone show her husband?"

Annie nodded. "Doc Dan was a favorite among all the nurses. Once he kicked that tramp out, he made the fastest recovery ever. He divorced her for adultery, said the cost of getting rid of her was worth every penny."

Sarah sent a furtive glance over at the couple. Was that the type of woman Tanner wanted? A woman he couldn't trust? If that was the case, she needed to stop fantasizing about someone she would never have. "Do you think Tanner knows about it?" Annie's laughter drew her attention.

"Tanner could easily have been one of the guys sleeping around with her at the time."

"Well, I'd have to hear him admit to it before I believed something like that. He's a friend and I like to give my friends the benefit of the doubt."

Annie shrugged before digging into her stuffed shrimp. "Just more proof that you're much too nice of a person to be hanging with the likes of me."

"Oh right, like you're so jaded."

"Only toward sex-on-the-brain-womanizers who haven't proven they can do any better yet. I've got a history with that guy during the Tiffany-Tanner era." She held one hand up. "I'm not getting into details here—it'll ruin my appetite, and I can't remember the last time I ate food this good. Between the heartburn during pregnancy and two months of breastfeeding, it seems like forever since I've eaten anything seasoned or fried."

Sarah welcomed the change of subject. "No problems transitioning baby boy to the formula and bottle feeding?" She dug into her own crawfish etouffee over angel hair pasta, savoring every bite of the tasty Cajun dish. "God, this is so good."

"I know, right? This place has never failed me yet." Annie dabbed at her mouth with her napkin. "Jake took to the bottle like a miniature hoover. Tiffany's tips on weaning him over a week or so helped. How about your twins? Did they have trouble adjusting to formula?"

"If you'll remember, they didn't have much of a choice. Their father made sure of that." Sarah still had nightmares about the five days she and her baby girls had spent locked up in Troy's bedroom. With no food to sustain her, she'd quit producing breast milk on the fourth day. By the time they were rescued, she'd dropped over ten pounds and her daughters were hungry enough to take to any formula.

Annie's hand flew to her mouth. "I'm so sorry, Sarah! I'm such a ditz sometimes. I'd forgotten—"

Sarah waved her fork, interrupting her friend's apology. "Don't worry about it. Honestly, I hardly think about it at all. Besides, if it hadn't happened, I would never have met any of you. Knowing you all has been such a blessing to my babies and me. I can't get myself to regret any of it."

Even the death of my daughters' father.

She sent a silent plea for forgiveness at the thought, though she couldn't help but remember Troy at his worst. The man was mean, controlling, dangerous, and damned near impossible to avoid. Even so, she hadn't wanted him dead—just out of their lives. She often wondered if he regretted anything before he drowned on that stormy night in the Gulf of Mexico.

"Earth to Sarah! Do you read?"

Sarah blinked as Annie waved her hand in front of her face. "Sorry, guess my mind wandered off for a bit. Did I miss something?"

"Um…only the fact that Mr. Collins, over there, keeps craning his neck when his hussy date isn't watching to look in this direction, and I know damn well it's not to see me.

You two don't have something going on, do you?"

"I've only spoken to him a few times. Angelique brought him over to meet me right before I went to work with her. During the visit, he discovered the twins had cut their first teeth. He came back a week or so later to bring the girls a couple of adorable outfits."

"Was he alone when he brought them?"

Sarah adjusted the napkin on her lap as their waitress refilled her tea. "Mm, I believe he was. Could you pass me a package of sweetener, please?" She caught the look of amusement Annie sent her way. "What? He dropped off the clothes and left. End of story," she said, sounding snarkier than she'd intended, even to her own ears.

Annie's brow rose as she lifted her glass of tea. "I didn't say a thing."

∿

Sarah pushed past the restaurant door out into the midday mist and drizzle of the late winter's day. Though spring was just around the corner, the unusually cooler temps weren't quite ready to surrender to this area of southwest Louisiana. She pulled her sweater tightly around her, staring out at the dampened parking lot as she waited for Annie to join her. In seconds she heard the door opening behind her. "God, Annie, do you think this dreary weather will ever end?"

"It's supposed to clear up and get warmer by tomorrow, I hear."

She spun around at the tantalizingly familiar sound of Tanner's voice. Shocked speechless, she pressed her hand to her abdomen, her stomach churning with butterflies at the sight of him. She stared stupidly up at the man, unable to come up with a single comment to start a conversation. Thankfully, he wasn't as dumbstruck.

"How've you been, Sarah? Are the twins well?"

The sound of a horn blast from behind jarred her from her stupor. "Fine! I've been fine, and so are the girls."

"Good, I bet they've grown a lot since I've seen them last." He flashed a brilliant smile.

"They're growing so fast, trying to crawl. It won't be long before they'll be getting into everything." She laughed nervously as he smiled down at her. "Is that a new girlfriend—I mean—how've *you* been?" She snapped her mouth shut, wishing she could materialize into one of those roly-poly pill bugs. That way she could close herself up and roll right on out of this conversation. She squeezed her eyes shut. "God, that was so rude of me. I'm sorry, Tanner."

He laughed and shook his head. "Not a girlfriend. She's just an old acquaintance. I've been okay, busy at the hospital, of course."

"Of course, working medical miracles and saving lives." She fidgeted and pushed her forever-escaping lock of hair behind her ear. Sadly, no type of mousse, gel, super-duper hold hairspray, clip, barrette, nor elastic band had been created that could keep that one stubborn strand from ruining an otherwise perfectly arranged hairdo. She glanced up as Tanner's 'acquaintance' stepped through the doorway, perfectly arranged and not a hair out of place.

The woman, obviously a master at multi-tasking, took no longer than two seconds to latch onto Tanner's arm, thereby establishing possession. Her one critical glance in Sarah's direction instantaneously judged her comparably dowdy presence, deemed her an unworthy opponent, and cast her aside without a second thought. It was a subtle, yet totally effective attack on Sarah's already lacking self-esteem.

Tanner gently detached the woman's claws from his arm so he could place a hand on the small of her back. "Yvette, I'd like you to meet a friend of mine. This is—"

"Tanner love, I really don't have time for introductions. I told you, I'm in a rush. I'm meeting with my designer and Coco waits for no one. *Ciao*, darling." Yvette locked her lips onto Tanner's while running her perfectly manicured nails softly over his crotch area.

He pushed at her hand and turned away, trying to escape the kiss. Sarah averted her gaze, embarrassed at the woman's blatant attempt to 'claim' her territory.

Tanner cleared his throat, obviously annoyed. "Wouldn't want you to be late to that meeting, Yvette. I'll be here, catching up with Sarah…a friend…a *nice* friend." Once she'd gained some distance he added. "Not that you'd recognize nice if it knocked you on your skinny little ass."

Sarah waited until he faced her to speak. "Lovely girl, Tanner…such nice manners."

"Sorry about that," he gave his head a shake. She's always been a spiteful bitch, but it's never bothered me—"

"Until now?"

His gaze settled on her, and he smiled. Not one of those half smiles of convenience to throw people off, the kind she'd perfected living with an abusive ex-husband, but one that allowed the sparkle to reach his gorgeous blue eyes.

"Forget her," he said with a wave of his hand. "Seriously, I don't doubt that the girls are thriving under your care, but how've you been, Sarah? No residual after effects from everything you went through? No bad dreams to haunt you?"

She gave him a casual single shoulder shrug. "Comes with the territory, I guess. My shrink assures me it'll go away with some time."

"I'm sure it will. You're surrounded by good people."

She met his kind gaze. "You seem like good people, too."

Laughter rumbled deep in his chest. "Not quite, but I'm trying to be."

Sarah stared off into the direction of Yvette, pulling her BMW out of the parking space like she was being chased by the devil himself, with no heed to any other vehicle around her. She faced Tanner again. "You *could* start by surrounding yourself with nicer people."

He stared down at her, his intense blue eyed gaze never wavering. "I was just thinking the same thing myself."

Chapter 2

"Dr. Collins, please report immediately to the ER...Dr. Tanner Collins to the ER..."

Tanner chugged the rest of his V-8 and threw the can in the recycling bin on his way out of the doctor's lounge, hoping the ER case was nothing too serious.

He entered the room to adrenaline pumping chaos...broken bones, severe cuts, and a toddler with all the signs of severe brain trauma. A family of four hit by a carload of drunken teenagers, driven by a slightly less inebriated designated driver who'd run a traffic light.

After six grueling hours of surgery on the infant, he pushed past his exhaustion to speak with the family members gathered in the surgical waiting room. The grandparents, both of whom he recognized as members of the same Mardi Gras Krewe he belonged to, came rushing up as soon as he entered the room.

"Dr. Collins, do you have any news for us?" she pleaded.

Tanner stared down into eyes the same shade of blue as her granddaughter's, dreading what he had to report to this poor woman and her husband. He clasped the grandmother's hand, his chest already aching with sadness. "I'm so sorry, Mrs. Meredith. We tried everything possible to save your granddaughter, but there was just far too much trauma to the brain. We're doing all we can now to insure your daughter retains her cognitive functions.

He stood back as she crumbled into her husband's embrace. Within moments they were surrounded by family and friends, leaving Tanner an opening to back slowly out of the room. Re-entering the surgical ward, he cast one more glance at the devastated family before letting the door swing closed with a quiet swoosh.

He stood for a moment, pressing the palms of his hands over his eyes, wondering if he could have done anything differently to save the child's life. A gentle touch to his shoulder brought his head around.

"There are some things you can't change, Tanner."

He faced Tiffany McAllister, whose soft brown eyes reflected her sorrow. He covered her hand with his own and stared down at the ex-fiancé he now considered a wonderful friend. "I know, Tiff…but dammit, kids are the worst. Man, I hate losing babies, and I detest having to tell the family."

Her head cocked slightly at his last comment. "You used to make the nurses do it for you—said it enabled you to avoid family drama and get more work done. I always suspected it was to keep from getting emotional."

He pushed playfully at her shoulder. "I'm not emotional, Dr. McAllister. Just regretful I couldn't do more."

"You can't fool me, Dr. God's gift to womankind." She gave his chest a playful poke with her finger. "I always suspected you had a good heart lurking somewhere in there. I know you're beating yourself up over this, wondering what you should have done differently. I observed that surgery, you know. The entire team did everything right. It just wasn't meant to be."

"I know you're right—here," he said, tapping his head. He lowered his hand to place it on his chest. "Somewhere along the way from there to here, I lose the certainty."

"If you didn't, you'd be speaking in computer code, Tanner. That's what enables us to sympathize and empathize. Families don't ever want to hear they've lost someone they love, but imagine how insignificant they'd feel having to hear it from a robot or a computer screen. We can't lose our humanity to progress. You showed them yours by telling them yourself."

He nodded in reluctant acceptance and followed her down the corridor.

～

Hours later, exhausted and tense, he entered his apartment just as his cell phone chirped with an incoming text. The emptiness of his spacious apartment was too much to handle. He flipped on the big screen and dropped the remote on the couch. Soft country music flowed from the speakers. He remembered his friend, Angelique Baptiste, programming his satellite station to country during her last brief, though energetic, visit. She'd stopped by to tell him she and Mike were going to Dallas for the week and dropped off several houseplants. He still hadn't figured out how he'd ended up being her personal plant sitter.   Angel had barged inside with armloads of Ivy, African Violets, and Tea Roses. She'd proceeded to tell him he had the most room and the best southern exposure of any of her friends. Didn't ask, just insisted she knew he was capable of not killing her precious plants. She'd stayed long enough to have one K-cup of decaf coffee and zipped out, leaving instructions on how and when to water.

Tanner kicked off his trainers and dropped to the couch, pulling his phone from the pocket of his scrubs. Simone Taylor's name flashed across the screen and he pulled up her message, with the subject titled "URGENT!"

Hlo baby! Jst trtd mslf to 2 pcs of fdg and divinity. Nd pc of anthr kind...sugr mstve gn str8t to my libido! Up to a L8 pm boo-tay call?
S

"S?" he mumbled, shaking his head. "God forbid she type out her entire name." But then, why would she bother to do that when the entire message was a hodge-podge of fragmented words.   He'd complained to her before, insisting her shortcut texting took him five times longer to read. She'd given him a blank look, saying, "And your point is *what* exactly?"

He dropped his head back on the couch, considering whether, or not a visit from his latest go-to-nympho would do the trick for him tonight.

Just as he'd talked himself into it, a country version of an old seventies pop hit stopped him from taking her up on the offer.

Jimmy Wayne belting out "Sara Smile" never failed to bring up the image of soft brown eyes, silken curls, and dimples.

The thought of this particular Sarah curbed his appetite for any other woman.

He raised the volume and stretched out on his leather couch, eyes closed, and foot tapping the air to the song that reminded him of her. As soon as it finished, he lifted the phone and answered the text with a brief 'Not tonight'. He grimaced when, almost immediately, she answered back with 'Y not?'

He frowned, wondering how she'd handle the truth—*Because you're not her.* Instead, he answered with a generic 'Need sleep'. He hit send, received an animated sad face emoticon in reply, and dropped his phone on the carpet.

"I'm getting too old for this shit," he groaned, rolling over onto his side, his face against the back of the padded, high-grade leather. With the song still bouncing around in his head, and drowsy from exhaustion and a long day of surgeries, he fell asleep.

He didn't know whether to thank a rare episode of good karma or the grace of God, but he dreamed of Sarah. His fingers flexed, then closed, wrapping around the silky softness of curls highlighted with streaks of gold. She'd just raised her mouth to his for a kiss, her passion infused pink lips smiling, speaking his name softly. She repeated it, over, and over, getting gradually louder…more insistent.

"Tanner!"

He wrenched to the side and took a short nose dive from the comfort of his couch to the hard, cold floor.

"Shit!"

"Tanner! Open the door! I know you're in there."

He jerked up, banging his elbow on the end table. "Son of a..."

"Tanner!"

"Wait a damn minute!" he called out, annoyed as hell and in pain, not to mention sexually frustrated, and exhausted. He dug his phone out from under his hip and checked the time. "Midnight?"

Pulling himself to his feet, he rubbed his hand over his face and stumbled to the door to yank it open. "What the hell, Simone? What part of 'Need sleep' did you not understand?"

The petite blonde curled herself around him, planting both hands on his butt cheeks and grinding herself against him. "Oh, don't be mad at me, baby. I tried to go to sleep...I truly did, but I'm too horny. Turns out it's justified. A friend of mine just told me that chocolate fudge and divinity eaten together act as an aphrodisiac. Now who would have known that?"

"Somehow I doubt your fact source, but what I do know is that when you're on a quest for sex, you'll say damn near anything to get it."

"It's true, Tan. Let me start up your laptop and I'll show you on the internet."

"And everyone knows if it's on the net it's true, right?"

"Well, maybe not everything, but this is has been scientifically proven."

"Come on, Simone. Surely you don't believe that shit, do you?"

Simone pouted prettily, rubbing her hand along his thigh, upward toward his crotch. "How about if we come up with another way to prove it to you? Why don't you let me climb right on up to this laptop, right...*here*," she said, latching onto him through his thin scrub pants.

He sucked in his breath at the feel of her hand wrapped around him. She lifted his shirt simultaneously to bare his chest to her hungry mouth.

"Simone!" he hissed, more annoyed than turned on,

which in itself was strange. "What did you do all day?"

"I skipped one class to do some shopping, and then skipped another to take a nap. I wanted to get to the club early, only you weren't *there*..." she whined.

"Because I was in surgery all day, not shopping and sleeping, dammit! I work for a living, Simone. You know, in a hospital...operating on people who've been in accidents. Like entire families who've been hit by a bunch of kids riding around drunk in their daddy's car. By the way, the blood alcohol level of their designated driver was probably lower than yours is now."

"Don't be such a downer, baby. I'm sure you patched everybody up just fine," she purred, rubbing her palm firmly against him.

"No," he growled, and yanked her hand away. "I didn't. As a matter of fact, a ten month old baby girl died on my table during the surgery. But hopefully, we kept the thirty-year-old mother of two...well, one now...from having permanent brain damage so she can recognize her broken-hearted husband and three-year-old son after losing her daughter."

Simone stared at him as though he'd suddenly turned into a complete stranger. She sighed with resignation and rolled her eyes.

"Bummer."

He clenched his jaw tightly, grinding out the one word he could manage without a curse attached to it. "Go."

She pulled back a diamond-clad hand, and fluttered her eyelashes coated with mascara. "You can't be serious!"

Tanner held open the door and gave her a gentle, but firm nudge toward the opening. "I'm serious. I can call you a cab, but I'd prefer you wait in your own car so I can get back to sleep. I've got patients to attend in the morning."

"I'm not drunk, you asshole. But I *am* pissed!" She stepped out onto the stoop and turned back to face him, flourishing her hand along the length of her skin tight designer jeans. "Hope your taste buds have a long memory, buddy, because you will never get a taste of this again."

"I find my taste has changed in a lot of things lately. Don't take it personally, Simone. It's long overdue—but I've finally realized how futile it is to resist." He raised his arms and let them drop to his sides. "Sooner or later, we all have to grow up." Tanner couldn't help but laugh as her face took on the characteristics of someone who'd just sucked on a green persimmon.

"I don't wanna grow up, and they can't make me," she said, shaking her fist dramatically at an invisible enemy. She crossed her arms across her chest and finally cracked a big grin at Tanner.

"Still mad at me?" he asked.

"Nah, I can't stay mad at you. Every girl needs at least one older lover in her life. Someone I can think about fondly...years from now... when I see your obituary in the paper—"

"Arrgh! If I can just...get...this...out!" he said, pulling at an imaginary stake in his heart. He joined in her laughter, shaking his head. "Just more proof that I can't keep up with you."

She sobered, took a step forward, and gently caressed his face. "Just because you don't want to anymore, doesn't mean you can't." She rose to her tiptoes and planted a kiss firmly on his lips. "Goodbye Tanner. Just remember, if your new taste fails to satisfy that voracious appetite of yours, I'm only a text message away."

He bowed at the waist. "Goodbye, Simone. I wish you the best."

Chapter 3

Tanner pushed Angelique's doorbell then took a knee to retie his loosened shoelace. When the door creaked open he spoke without looking up. "I hope red goes with whatever we're having, since you guys didn't tell me what was on the menu."

"I don't think Angelique figured it out until a couple of hours ago, but if you're talking about wine, I'm sure red will do."

Tanner paused at the totally unexpected sound of Sarah's voice. He glanced up, seeing her curious gaze trained on him. "I didn't expect to see you here."

She gave him a tentative smile. "Same here. It's been awhile, hasn't it? What've you been up to?"

He stood, handing her the bottle of merlot. "Depends…what've you heard?"

Her laughter rang through the space, sounding much lighter, more carefree than he remembered, but why wouldn't it be? She wasn't faced with looking over her shoulder and hiding from an abusive husband for the rest of her life.

"I don't need to ask how you are. You look fantastic." She did, too, having finally gained back enough weight to make her look fit instead of frail. Her cheeks were flushed a bright pink, a color that definitely looked good on her. Though he'd like to claim credit for it, if he was to guess, he'd say alcohol played a part in it.

"Thank you. I feel fantastic." She ushered him inside and picked up a half filled crystal wine glass. She raised it to eye level. "A couple more of these and I'll really feel good," she giggled.

"Did somebody get a reprieve from being a hard-working mom for the night?"

She gave him a thumbs-up. "Not just the night, but the entire weekend! Leah and Daniel practically packed a bag for me and pushed my butt out the door. They made reservations for me at a swanky hotel here in Lafayette, and said they didn't want to see my face until Sunday afternoon. I'm on vacation for the first time since my babies were born!"

Angelique entered the room, carrying a tray of cheese, crackers, bite-sized pieces of Andouille sausage, and smoked boudin, sliced into two-inch sections. "And who did she decide to visit first? Me—the woman who drove her crazy while training her for her job for two weeks." She set the tray down on the cocktail table and threw one arm around Sarah's shoulders. "And boy, am I glad she did." She planted a loud kiss on Sarah's cheek before the two of them burst into giggles.

Tanner snorted. "Both of you are on your way to shit-faced drunk. Please tell me Harper's here, or I'll have to shoot myself."

"He's taking the rest of the boudin off the pit. And shit-faced is entirely possible." She retrieved a glass from the cloth covered buffet she'd set up as a makeshift bar area. "That's the benefits of having this supper at my house. I don't have to worry about getting home. I've already told Sarah if she's tipsy she can stay here for the night. Unless you—" she said with emphasis, while jabbing a finger in Tanner's face. "—want to be the sobering influence and drive her back to her hotel."

He nodded, watching Sarah dance barefoot on the plush rug to country music playing softly from Angel's sound system. "That's a possibility. I'll hold it to one glass of wine, in case she decides she needs me."

The sound of Angel clearing her throat got his attention. He had to chuckle at the dark look of warning she wore. "To drive her to her hotel, Ang. That's all."

"Hmph! That better be all." She sidled up next to him and spoke in a voice low and menacing. "I'm warning you now, Tanner. You hurt that girl, and I'll get an old Voodoo priestess I know in New Orleans to put the *gris-gris* on you—guaranteed to shrivel your nuts to the size of two itty-bitty raisins." She held up two fingers pinched closely, for emphasis.

Tanner grabbed her hand and lowered it. "Calm down, Marie Laveau. She's not my type." He turned, deciding even the company of Mike Harper, was better than two tipsy women and Angie's suspicious mind.

"Not yet, anyway," she said.

The last thing he heard as he headed to her patio was another round of her drunken giggles accompanied by slightly off-key singing.

∾

Sarah leaned back in her chair and placed both hands on her belly. "The lasagna was delicious, but I can't eat another bite."

"As long as you eat enough to absorb some of that alcohol," Tanner said. "You sure as hell don't need to be hung over and sick during your first personal vacation since you've given birth."

"You know, now that I think of it, I've never had a hangover," she said, sipping from her water glass. "It makes me wonder what other kinds of things I missed out on."

Mike Harper, Angelique's fiancé, swigged from his beer bottle and set it down. "You mean like the bubonic plague and scurvy?"

Tanner nodded. "Or tuberculosis and cholera?"

She waved them off. "Nooo...I mean like going on spring break in Florida or camping in a cabin in the woods with a bunch of girlfriends."

"Hmm...spring break sounds good, but that cabin in the woods thing sounds like the perfect setting for a slasher movie." Angel grasped the large bread knife and waved it in the air.

"Yeah, complete with a hockey mask wearing guy who's recently escaped from a hospital for the criminally insane," Tanner added, throwing a paper napkin over his face with three holes torn out for his eyes and mouth.

"During a horrendous storm," Mike threw in.

"Yeah, the kind that knocks out all the power, including the phone lines, of course." Tanner blew the napkin off his face. "Come to think of it, I believe I saw that flick."

Sarah sobered, thinking of a particular dream she'd had once, when Troy was still on the loose and out to get her. "None of that stuff scares me," she admitted. *Not after what I've gone through.*

Angelique hiccupped and covered her mouth. "Es'cuse me. We're trying to tell you that if you've never experienced a hangover, consider yourself lucky."

"I'm sure you're right," Sarah said. "I guess the part that sounds so appealing is the ability to cut loose and not think of the consequences for a change. It seems like I've been taking care of people since I was thirteen years old."

Tanner rested his arms on the table and leaned in, obviously interested in hearing what she had to say. "Your parents both passed when you were younger, right?"

She nodded. "My mom went first, after a two year battle with cancer. Mom's death was hard on all of us, but she and dad were so close; I think it must have been hardest on him. He lost the only woman he'd ever loved, when they were both barely into their forties. There were days when I know dad wouldn't have eaten a thing if I hadn't been there, coaxing him along. He lost interest in everything without her around."

A sniff from Angelique had Sarah pulling away from the memories to cast several glances at the others, all of whose eyes swam with sympathetic understanding. "Don't get me wrong, I wasn't neglected physically. It's just that it's extremely difficult to live in the same house with someone who's hopelessly heartbroken."

Angie wiped the tears from the corner of her eyes. "Your parents sound a lot mine, Sarah. It would have devastated either of them to lose the other." She smiled at her fiancé as Mike snorted in enthusiastic agreement.

"Good Lord, yes! It's obvious that those two are still 'ate up' with each other." He lifted Angie's hand to his mouth for a kiss. "Just like we will be at that age, babe."

Sarah smiled longingly at the couple. "I can believe that." She sighed again, allowing herself to speak openly of her greatest sorrow. "Lord, I wish my girls could have known their grandparents." A subtle movement from Tanner caught her attention and she found herself studying his suddenly uncomfortable demeanor.

Angel pushed back from the table to grab a bottle of wine. "Let's retire to the parlor, shall we?" she said, adapting an air of aristocracy.

Sarah picked up her glass and followed her friend into the living room.

∾∾

Tanner spent the next hour trying to act as though he didn't give a shit. Not about how Sarah's eyes sparkled when she cut loose and laughed with the aid of a little wine. Not how the sunlight from the bay window cast occasional glimmers of light onto her golden locks. Definitely not how her hips, wrapped in snug jeans, swayed gently to the music piped out from speakers.

He hadn't seen her drink much since he'd arrived on the scene, but she obviously had a low tolerance for alcohol. It was nice to see her relaxed and actually laughing—smiling, without her usual trace of haunted wariness. He wondered how much time would have to pass before she'd truly feel free again.

Sarah jumped up and grabbed the remote to raise the volume on the surround sound. "Okay, somebody has to dance with me to this song," she said, as Jimmy Wayne began crooning "Sara Smile".

"Mmm, I love you, but not enough to give up my dance partner," Angelique said, latching tightly to her fiancé. She aimed a look at Tanner.

Tanner set down his glass of iced water and stood with his hand outstretched and smiling down at her. "I guess it's up to me then."

An hour earlier, he and Mike had pulled the sofa back to free up more floor space for dancing. Up until now, Tanner had avoided the dance floor. Tired of hearing his excuse that he didn't dance to Cajun or Zydeco music, Angel had recently switched to a country ballad station.

Well hell, if he was going to do it, he may as well do it the right way. He closed his fingers over Sarah's and tugged her to him. Her breath caught in a delighted gasp as he whirled her skillfully into the spacious center area of the room. Tanner couldn't help but laugh at the shock registering on her face.

"Surprise," he said.

She closed her mouth with a snap. "I thought you said you couldn't dance."

"I *can't* dance to zydeco music, but anything else is fair game."

"You should have said something sooner. We could have changed the station before now."

He gave her a casual shrug. "Not a big deal, Sarah. You were having a good time, and now…" he tightened his hold on her lower back to spin her a few times to the music, "…it's my turn."

Her head fell back. Eyes closed, she hummed to the melody. Soon she was singing along to the lyrics, harmonizing nicely with the country artist.

"I've always loved this song. Even if my name wasn't Sarah, I'd still love it."

She cracked one of her lids open and frowned. "You don't look like you believe me, but it's true. I've always been a huge fan of…" Her voice faded and the look on her face revealed a mixture of confusion and annoyance. "Damn if I can remember who sings this."

"Haulin' ass," he said.

"That's it! No. Wait…" She stared up at him, her brow scrunched. "What'd you say?"

He burst into laughter at her total loss of concentration. "Jimmy Wayne sings this country version, but Hall and Oates sang the original, way back before you were born. One of my buddies had their greatest hits cd, and somebody in the group started calling them "Haulin' Ass" instead of Hall and Oates." He raised his hands and dropped them unceremoniously. "What can I say? We were twelve and thought we were getting away with something massive."

"Teenage boys are such idiots."

He nodded and grinned. "I'd like to disagree with you, but it'd be pointless. We were total idiots—all of that burgeoning testosterone and not an iota of sense."

"What was the deal with popping bra straps?" she asked. "Seriously…what could possibly have turned guys on about hearing the pop of a girl's training bra?"

He burst into laughter. "Hell, I don't know. I think it's some kind of male bonding tradition. I'm sure girls did equally stupid things during those mysterious sleep overs y'all were always having."

"I never went to any of those sleep overs."

"Is that your way of getting out of answering? You mean after all these years you're still sworn to secrecy?" He chuckled.

Her smile faded as she pondered his statement. "My mom starting getting ill when I was twelve. Her doctor insisted it was anemia for a year. After that is when dad finally convinced her to go to a specialist in New Orleans. By then the cancer was in latter stage three. Two years later she was dead. The point being, that I was needed at home."

"That's a serious load for a teenager to bear. Seems like you should have gotten out at least every once in a while," he said, remembering how irresponsible and self-centered he'd been toward his own parents at that age.

Her brow furrowed as she shook her head slowly. "You don't understand how difficult it was to leave her to even go to school in the mornings. I always had this fear that by the time I got home, she'd be gone. I didn't *want* to leave her…ever."

Tanner fought to keep from pulling her tightly into his

arms. Instead he applied a gentle pressure to her lower back. "I'm sorry." Suddenly all he wanted was to make her smile. *Sara...Sarah...Smile.*

"It's okay...and uh...did you realize the song is over?"

"Oh...yeah...it is, isn't it?" What was it about this girl that made him feel like an awkward thirteen-year-old kid? The only thing missing was the uncontrollable wood that was destined to pop up at the most inconvenient times. The opening notes of another ballad allowed him to keep from breaking his hold on her. "Want to go again?"

She smiled up at him. "Sure."

After several seconds, Tanner pushed on. "After what you've been through with your ex, nobody would blame you if you swore off men forever." Her light-hearted laughter gave him reason to hope.

"I can't bring myself to blame a whole gender for one man's screw-ups. Besides, I can't say I wasn't warned off of him. He was the town bad-boy...and I had to be the one woman who'd change him. Ugh!"

Tanner attempted to stifle the longing in his gut as she lifted her beautiful eyes to his.

"Ya see, girls are idiots too, just in different ways." She turned her head to the side and smiled. "Maybe one day I'll try dating again, if I can find somebody that fits my criteria. He'll have to be good daddy material, as well as good husband material. I don't have the luxury of *impulse shopping* anymore, Tanner. There are two other lives I'm responsible for."

Stiff-backed and suddenly more aware of the situation than ever before, Tanner finished the dance without saying another word. A minute later, he peeked at his phone, saying he had to get to the hospital, and got the hell out of there as quickly as he could. As much as he hated leaving her side, he knew he was nowhere close to being the type of man she needed in her life.

Chapter 4

Tanner exited the fifth floor elevator and headed toward ICU, avoiding the curious gazes of the night staff. He could well imagine them asking each other what the hell he was doing there. He'd fled Sarah's company, too afraid she'd discover that he didn't fit any of the criteria as husband or father material. Did he want to fit? Hell, he had to admit the jury was still out on that one. So, he'd ended up here at the hospital, when he wasn't even on call. Part of him knew he just didn't want to lie to Sarah. He'd said they needed him back at the hospital, so here he was.

He checked on the two patients he'd performed surgery on the day before. Both were fine, recuperating at the expected rate and neither showing signs of complications. *Of course,* he added, sounding smug, even in his own mind.

Bored and hoping to find some kind of stimulation for his mind, as well as his body, he headed down the staff elevator to the emergency room. He couldn't help but smile as he remembered something his Aunt Betsy had told him when he was just a kid. *"Tanner, my boy, making yourself useful is the easiest way to stay out of trouble. Now, go wash my car for me."*

His father had been furious at his sister for demeaning his son to the task of menial labor, but he'd enjoyed having an excuse to get wet and dirty. Aunt Betsy had been the black sheep of his father's side of the family and was hardly ever spoken of, much less visited. Even now, he couldn't imagine why his father had gone, much less why he'd brought him along for the visit. His mother had always referred to her as the "...only member of your father's family who refuses to accept her station in life." Looking back on it, he now realized that she was probably the only one in the family who knew that just being rich didn't necessarily make you better.

As the elevator doors opened with a quiet swoosh, Tanner made a mental note to look up his rebel aunt. He took one step and froze, at once wary of the unnaturally eerie silence in the emergency room. At first glance, nothing looked unusual. He took a second cautious step forward and caught the terrified gaze of one of the ER nurses. He stood immobile, seeing her eyes dart frantically from him to an area just out of his line of sight. He eased his way slowly along the edge of the wall to hide behind a rack full of medical supplies. A cautious peek around it brought the situation to light.

A young man stood with a hand-gun pointed shakily at...who? He craned his neck, hoping to glean some kind of information. Finally the man spoke, his voice gravelly and full of pain.

"Look lady, I don't want to hurt you, but I need something...I...I just need the pain to go away!"

"It's withdrawal symptoms, sir. Please, put the gun down and let us admit you. We can help."

Tanner winced, hearing the voice of Rozalyn Bradley, the longest employed nurse in the hospital. Longest employed, which was code for oldest, most crotchety, and otherwise long-out-of-patience nurse in any ward. Roz was in her early to mid-sixties and approaching retirement age. As it stood, he could hear the restraint in her tone, knowing the toll it must be taking on her not to unleash her infamous verbal whoop-ass on him. The woman could be truly terrifying to those unfortunates incurring her wrath.

He backed off long enough to send a quick text to the security guards, explaining the volatile situation. The last thing they needed was the blare of sirens or anything to incite the man to lose what little composure he had.

He turned off his phone so as not to call attention to himself, then took a breath and peered around the corner again. The guy paced erratically across the room, waving the pistol haphazardly from one side to the other.

"Come *on*!" he screamed. "I *know* you have something in this damn place. You!" he said, pointing the pistol at the nurse in Tanner's line of sight. "Get me something...Now! Or else *she's* dead!" He swung his arm around to jam the barrel against Rozalyn's skull.

The wild-eyed nurse held out one hand. "Okay! I'll find something. Just please don't hurt her." She side-stepped to the rack where Tanner hid and acted like she was searching for something.

"Lure him over here," Tanner mouthed when her terrified gaze found his through the gaps in shelving. She gave him a barely perceptible nod before latching onto a vial of something that could have passed for drugs.

"Here! This is codeine and it'll help with the pain."

"Give it to me!" The junkie rushed toward her to grab for the bottle. He clutched at the bottle with both hands, trying to decipher its contents.

Tanner took the opportunity to grab him from behind, simple since he was distracted by the promise of drugs. In one quick motion, he grabbed the gun, holding it well out of reach from the man, who was actually no more than a kid, barely in his twenties. Weak and shaky from his addiction, his resistance to Tanner ended in a few seconds.

"God!" He clutched his stomach. "Please! Help me!"

"We will." Tanner searched the relief filled faces of the other occupants of the room. "Is everyone all right?"

Rozalyn wiped her brow and nodded. "Now I am. I never thought I'd be pleased to see *you*, Doctor Collins."

"Careful, Roz...you'll make me blush," Tanner snorted to the woman he'd had a loathe/hate relationship with over the last ten years. "Seriously, is everyone okay?"

She nodded. "They should be. I'm the only one old enough to have a heart attack from the stress and I'm fine. Thank you, Doctor Collins."

"You're welcome. I can take care of this if you want to take a breather."

She placed her fists on her hips. "And have you report that I'm not fit to do my job? Oh, hell, no!"

Tanner smiled down at the tiny, but spirited, black woman whose single braid of gray hair had begun to come loose from the perpetual bun. It had always looked like a snake, ready to uncoil and strike at any moment. "Come on, Roz. You know I wouldn't do that, don't you?"

She lifted her chin, perusing him over the rim of her glasses. "Hmph…I guess I'll have to take your word for it, seeing as how you're the hero of the hospital and all."

"Oh God, don't start," Tanner pleaded as he turned the young man over to one security guard and the gun over to the other. "I suspect we'll be getting him back for detox."

"What about now? Can't you give me something *now*?" The young man was nearly hysterical.

"Sorry, kid. If you'd come in without the gun he may have been able to help you," the security guard answered. "Now it's out of his hands. We have to wait for someone to pick you up for processing. It could take a while for you to make it back here."

Tanner shook his head as the guards left the room with their prisoner. He turned to Roz, wanting to tell her he wished he could have done something for the kid now. He froze. She leaned her head forward against the back wall of the elevator. He stepped inside and placed his hand on her shoulder.

"Roz, do you feel faint?" He checked her pulse at her wrist, relieved that it was normal. She lifted her gaze and he was surprised to find her eyes tearful, even though a smile lit her face.

"Oh, I'm fine Doc, I really am. It's just that, even at my age, I'm amazed that the good Lord still finds ways to surprise me. Imagine *you*…being the one to come in and keep that boy from shooting me, or himself, or anyone else in that room, dead as a door nail." He could sense her failed effort to keep the laughter from her voice.

Tanner stood back, arms crossed. "Well, hell Roz, don't hold back. Tell me how you *really* feel."

"I'm sorry," she gasped through her laughter.

More amused than annoyed, he continued. "No. No, I

don't think you are. Go on and tell me why you think I'm such a loser. Tell the world," he said, waving his hand at the curious onlookers.

Roz finally seemed to get hold of her emotions and took a deep breath, wiping her eyes with an embroidered handkerchief she pulled out of her pocket. "Oh, Doc Collins, that's the best laugh I've had in a while…a long while."

Tanner gave her a quick nod. "I'm glad I've finally managed to do something that meets your approval. Obviously, it's been a long time coming."

She looked around him at one of the other nurses. "Y'all got this for a while, Deb?"

"Yes ma'am. You go on, and take a break, Roz. If anyone needs one, it's you," the woman told her.

"I believe I *will* go take a break," she said, reaching around for the elevator pad. "I am plum exhausted from all that laughing." She grinned up at Tanner. "Come on up with me to get my thermos out of my locker. I'm in need of a real cup of coffee. Not that see-through crap they brew in our lounge. I'll even share, if you think you're man enough to handle it." She waited until the elevator doors closed before continuing.

"I looked at tonight's schedule for ER doctors on call and it sure wasn't our in-house brain surgeon. So, I can't help but wonder—what made you show up in the ER when you did?"

Tanner's mouth opened, then closed, and opened once more, though nothing came out.

"Pfft. Must be a woman." Roz spoke with finality.

He glared at her satisfied expression. "What makes you say that?"

"Only one thing could ever leave a self-absorbed letch like you speechless—and that's a woman." She crooked her head to look up at him. "How close am I?"

"You're—warm."

"Ah, come on, now, Doc. God hears even the whisper of a half-truth."

He rolled his eyes and looked away before releasing a loud sigh. "You're sitting right on the top of a roaring bonfire."

Rozalyn clapped her hands triumphantly. "And here I thought my instincts were beginning to dull."

The elevator doors opened and Tanner waited as Roz disappeared for a minute into the nurse's lounge then reappeared carrying an ancient steel thermos and one cup.

"Man, that's vintage," he said, eyeing the faded green bottle full of nicks and dents, as they seated themselves on a bench in front of the window.

"Was my daddy's," she said, lifting it for a quick inspection. "Just cause something gets old and ugly, it doesn't mean it's not useful. You kids are way too ready to throw out something you see as 'outdated' just to get a newer version of the same thing. What a damn waste."

Tanner accepted the cup from her and waited for her to uncap the thermos. "I can't argue with that, Roz. I'm on my fifth I-Phone when the first one did everything I needed it to."

She poured some of the dark brew into his cup while nodding. "I phones, tablets, computers, mp thingamajigs or whatever the hell they're called…all a bunch of bull shit, if you ask me. My granddaughter told me the other day she'd *shoot me a text* when she was ready for me to pick her up from her dance class. I told the little fart I'd be there at four p.m. and she'd damn well better have her butt there waiting for me, or I'd leave her like a no good husband."

Tanner tried to stifle the laugh, not even bothering to wonder if she was exaggerating.

"She's ten years old and typing on that little key pad like she came out of the womb attached to it. Last time she came for a visit I ripped it out of her hands and told her to pick up a damn book." She threw her head back and laughed. "Thought my high falutin' professor of a daughter-in-law would have a hissy fit over that, but they all put the damn things away until I'd had my visit with 'em, by God."

"Yeah, they've become extensions of us all, unfortunately. And texting—ugh, it's the worst. They don't even use whole words anymore, Roz. Everything's a shortcut, like LOL for laugh out loud."

She filled the thermos cover with coffee and took a sip. "Unless you're a senior, then it's short for 'Living on Lipitor'. BTW means 'Bring the Wheelchair'."

Tanner sputtered and choked on his coffee as Roz continued.

"You like that, Doc? How about WTF for 'Wet The Furniture' or DWI for 'Driving While Incontinent'? You want me to stop so you can catch your breath?"

Tanner held up his hand and gasped for air. "Yeah—please!" He coughed several times and finally managed to sober. "Where do you come up with this stuff, Roz?"

"You wouldn't believe me if I told you."

"Try me," he said, taking another sip of the strongest coffee he'd ever tasted.

"My eighty-two year old mother said her boy-friend emailed it to her."

Tanner jerked upright at her answer. "No!"

Roz nodded enthusiastically while lifting one hand high in the air. "Hand to God! She went down to the YWCA and took a class on basic computer and internet skills. Sat next to this man from Vinton and they've been emailing and Skype-ing each other ever since. Hell, I don't even *know* what it means to *Skype* somebody and I don't think I want to know, either. It sounds downright *nasty* to me!" She placed her hand on Tanner's arm. "Are you gonna make it, Doc?"

Tanner, still doubled over with laughter, finally managed to take a deep breath and speak. "Stop...Roz...You gotta stop!"

She chuckled. "You probably think I'm making this stuff up, but I swear I'm not. It's God's honest truth or may he strike me dead!"

"Oh, I believe you, and one of these days, I'd really like to meet your mother," he said, still wiping tears of laughter from his eyes.

Her broad smile reached all the way to warm brown eyes set in a face crinkled with laughter. "I never thought I'd be saying this to *you*, but I'd like you to meet her one day, too." She cocked her head curiously, pointing a finger at him. "Something or somebody has grabbed a hold of you. Now, what I want to know is why you're here on a big Saturday night instead of out acting the dog you normally are. Time to fess up, Doc."

Tanner took another sip of the strong brew then gave her a shrug. "No big deal, Roz. I wanted to check on a couple of patients."

"Like that adorable little girl who fell off the jungle gym this morning?"

He nodded. "Yeah, she's doing well…and the mother in that car accident two days ago…"

"You can't save everyone, Doc."

"I know, but it's hard to accept sometimes." He cleared his throat loudly. "Anyway, I couldn't sleep and found myself with nothing better to do. I decided to see if there was anything interesting in ER tonight. Turns out, there was." He sipped at his coffee again, feeling Roz's penetrating gaze on him, studying him, searching for flaws, no doubt

Roz spoke, her voice soft and penitent. "I'm beginning to think I've been too hard on you in the past."

He laughed and gave his head a slow shake. "Trust me, Roz. Whatever bad things you thought or said about me, you can bet your ass I had it coming."

"Maybe so, but that was the past. My old grandma said she could feel when people were changing for the better. Said their edges weren't as sharp. I never knew what she was talking about `til now. I can see it in you. Mind you, you aren't there, yet. You're still battling some demons, but you're getting there, Doc. You're getting there."

Chapter 5

Sarah eased the nursery door shut quietly behind her, breathing a sigh of relief when neither of the twins woke up crying again. She trudged wearily to the living room, throwing herself onto the cushy sofa for a short nap. Teething babies sure could put a strain on everyone within the range of them, and Sarah was no exception. Within seconds of settling into the soft cushions, the doorbell had her jumping up to answer it before it woke the twins again.

"Can I help you?" she asked the man who stood with his back to her, dressed in a crisply ironed burgundy shirt, tucked neatly into his dark blue, belted jeans. The sunlight caught light brown hair in a clipped short and neat style. He turned slowly and spoke.

"Hey, Sis. Long time no see, huh?"

Sarah's hand flew to her mouth as she took a step back. "Oh my God! Mitchell, is that you?"

He beamed at her, his face tanned and lined from years of serving in the war torn, middle-east's arid desert heat.

"Do you have another brother I don't know about?"

She flew into his open arms, laughing and crying simultaneously. "Why didn't you tell me you were coming?"

"I thought I did," he said, squeezing her tightly.

"Well, sure, a few months ago, but then they cancelled your leave."

"I told you I'd get here, didn't I? What'd I tell you about doubting me?" He held her at arm's length. "Man, let me get a good look at you, sis. You're too thin."

"*You're* the one that's too thin! Don't they feed you in the Marines?"

"I eat plenty. It's sweating my ass off over there that keeps it from sticking."

Sarah frowned, remembering the picture he'd sent a couple of years ago, all dressed in his camouflaged fatigues with full body armor and backpack. It didn't even take into account the weaponry he had to haul around, and all in dangerously debilitating heat.

"Are you sure you're okay?" She stepped back to get a good look at him. "No new wounds or scars you neglected to tell me about?"

"Nope, I'm still managing to dodge trouble."

"You'd better, you're the only family I have left and I worry about you."

"I know you do, and to tell you the truth, I have a decision to make…stay or go."

Her eyes clouded with tears at the thought of having her big brother permanently home. "Are you seriously considering leaving the military for good?"

"It's one possibility, Sis," he said, pulling her to him for another hug. "The only thing I know for sure is that I've got some heavy deliberating in my future."

∽⌒∾

Tanner filled a paper bag with hot-house tomatoes and paid the vendor before adding it to his wire handled basket. He turned in time to see Sarah leaning over a pile of cantaloupes, a smile plastered to her face as she closed her eyes to sniff the melons. Judging from the amount of items in her basket, she was obviously satisfied with the city's first farmers' market of the year.

Ready to call out to her, the greeting froze on his lips as a guy walked over to inspect her choices. Before long, he said something that had her throwing back her head in hysterical laughter. The mystery man threw his arm around her shoulders casually and turned her in the opposite direction.

"Tanner Collins…Calling Doctor Tanner Collins!"

He turned to see a busty, dark-eyed beauty staring up at him, arms crossed, booted foot tapping impatiently on the concrete. His mind worked frantically, trying to remember her name.

"I called out your name a couple of times, but you were too engrossed in the dark blond over there. Who is obviously one half of a couple," she added.

Too gorgeous to question whether or not he'd slept with her, Tanner tried to focus on the when and where of it. Knowing the answer would come to him soon, he stalled for time with a generic greeting that never failed.

"Well, hello, beautiful! How've *you* been?"

Her ear-to-ear grin revealed a beautiful set of deep-set dimples and straight, white teeth.

Dimples…Dimple…*Dimpled Darlene.*

"Tell me the truth, now. Do you even remember me?" she asked, one brow lifted at a provocative angle.

"I absolutely do remember you. How've you been, Darlene?"

"That was quite impressive, Tanner, but you can't fool me. I saw that panicky look guys get when they're suddenly face to face with a woman—desperately trying to remember her name and whether or not he slept with her."

"That's flawed reasoning, hon. I never doubted for a second that I'd spent some *quality* time with a looker like you."

"Oh, Mr. Smooth, just as I remember you," she said.

"It's the only way I know to be." He caught Sarah staring at him, her face a study of what she must be thinking of him. He swore silently, knowing it had to be anything but reputable.

～○

"We're not done yet, Sis. I've been dying for some fresh tomatoes," Mitch said, perusing the contents of her basket.

"I just saw some fabulous hot house tomatoes over this wa…"

Mitch took two steps forward before he realized he'd left Sarah behind. He turned back to see her gaze locked on something, or someone in the direction they were heading. Spinning around slowly, he studied the clean cut man, deep in conversation with a shapely brunette. The guy glanced in

Sarah's direction and froze, looking like he'd just been caught fraternizing in the enemy camp.

"You know him?" Mitch asked her, generally curious.

She nodded. "He's just a friend. I'm gonna go sit in the car with this stuff. You get your tomatoes and meet me when you're done."

He made his way back around to the other couple. He picked through a bunch of bright purple eggplant, remembering how much he liked them fried in cornmeal. He bagged a few of them before meandering over to the tomatoes, in the hope of picking up tidbits of conversation. He heard just enough to know they'd slept together in the not too distant past. The woman left, leaving Sarah's mystery man alone and searching the market...he presumed for his sister.

Mitchell cleared his throat to call attention to himself. "She's waiting for me in the car." Sarah's 'friend' swung around, obviously taken off guard.

"Excuse me?"

Mitchell extended his hand. "Mitch Hebert—Sarah's brother—and who the hell are you?"

"Tanner Collins," he said, taking Mitchell's hand in an equally strong grip. "I'm a friend of Sarah's."

"Really? You don't seem the type to be friends with my sister." He could tell he'd offended Collins by the subtle cock of his head.

"What type do you think I am?" he asked, his voice challenging, even though he was obviously curious to hear his answer.

"You are entirely too much of a lady's man, buddy. From the conversation with the leggy brunette, I don't see you turning it down very often."

"Eaves drop much?"

"If it keeps my sister from being hurt, you can bet your ass I'll do more than that. Listen, I don't know how much you know about Sarah, but she's gone through a rough time. She doesn't need anybody who won't be totally honest and loyal to her." He took a step closer.

"You got that?"

Tanner's back stiffened noticeably. "I know exactly what she's gone through. If this is big brother's way of telling me hands off—" He clutched his hand into a fist and let it fall loosely to his side. "It isn't necessary."

Mitch wondered at the man's tone of utter defeat. "And why is that?"

"Because, I *know* my limitations." Collins adjusted the bag of produce in his arms and backed away from him. "I know I'll never come close to being the kind of man Sarah wants or needs in her life. She deserves better than me." With one last nod of acknowledgement, he turned and walked away.

Mitch stood in the center aisle of the market, staring after Tanner Collins—more curious than ever about the man's feelings for his sister. In a scenario that should have been cut and dried simple, all he had was a shitload of unanswered questions. He headed back toward the car, thinking the situation called for a little reconnaissance, and who the hell could handle *that* better than a U.S. Marine?

∾

Tanner grabbed an apple from the bowl near the register and handed the waitress his card.

"Did you find everything to your satisfaction, sir?" the woman asked, giving him a look he knew too well.

"Lunch was fine, thanks—a good start to a long weekend." He'd been coming to this place for the occasional meal for years, but she'd only been here a couple of months. The café was easy walking distance from the hospital and served as a nice change from where he usually had lunch. After this morning's hectic schedule, followed by an unusually heavy load of surgeries, he had a craving for something more palatable than bland cafeteria food.

He gazed at the woman, noting the somewhat modest show of cleavage, and decided she was just the right mixture of down home southern girl and sophisticated vamp. The blond bombshell was probably working her way through college, and lucky for him, her tastes ran a little more toward men than boys.

She smiled, lowering her eyelashes seductively as she handed him his receipt, along with a card containing her name and contact info. He sent her a smile, adding a wink to let her know he appreciated the extra attention, especially since he was coming off of long, dry run in the sexual fulfillment department.

"Don't lose that," she purred, reaching over to flip the card and scribble the name of a club. "The DJ's slammin' and the bartender's my bestie." She slipped the card in his shirt pocket. "If you're lucky maybe you can take us both home tonight. My name's Charley, and I'll be there by ten."

He grinned noncommittally and left the café, debating on whether or not to throw the card away or take her up on it.

He pictured her, lids lowered and licking her plump, glossed lips and something stirred, tightening in an old familiar way. How long had it been? A month or more since he'd had sex? Sheesh, that was a friggin' eternity. He shook his head and walked to his silver Lexus, mumbling to himself the entire way.

∾

Mitch watched Collins walk outside, deliberate over the card and, wearing a shit-eating grin, slip it right back into his pocket. He sympathized with the poor bastard. If anybody knew how hard it was for a hound to ignore a scent once he discovered it, he did.

Once he removed his shades and caught the waitress' eye, it didn't take long for her to head toward the table he'd chosen…corner of the room with his back to the wall. Wearing civvies didn't stop him from being a cautious Marine.

"You ready to order now, good looking?" she said.

He flashed her, what the guys in his unit called his 'game on' smile. "Not quite yet, Miss, I'm still waiting on two others to join me, but I will take a coffee while I'm here, and uh…maybe you could suggest someplace where a guy like me could go to listen to some good music and drink a few beers. Maybe find some pretty lady to dance with."

"Well, this must be my lucky day, GI Joe. I know just the place."

"Guess the shorter hair gave me away." He waited as she wrote down some info on a napkin. He pocketed the info, hoping it was the same address she'd given Collins.

"Not so much the hair as the way you carry yourself," she said, leaving just long enough to return with a cup of coffee. "Free refills," she said, "And I'll be there by ten p.m."

"Live band or D.J.?"

"Slammin' D.J." she said.

"Good, I'll be there." Confident that he'd be able to start his surveillance on Collins soon, he placed the napkin in his wallet as Sarah and a gorgeous redhead approached the table.

"Hey, big brother, did somebody banish you to the corner of the room?" Sarah said, glancing at the empty tables around him.

"I like the corner, Sis, but we can move if it makes you uncomfortable."

The redhead piped up. "No, this is fine. It's a military thing, Sarah. They can't stand not to see what's going on behind them. Hi Mitchell, I'm Melanie Finley." She extended her hand. "My friends call me Mel, and boy have I heard a lot about you."

"The only Mel I've heard Sarah talk about is a cop. Is that you?"

"Afraid so." She bared straight, white teeth in a beautiful smile.

"Nice to meet you, Mel. So you live here in Lake Coburn?"

"No, I live in Lafayette but I try to come by at least once a week to see Sarah and the twins…and have lunch."

"How do you two know each other?" he asked,

genuinely interested.

"Uh…I guess I actually have Troy to thank for some good people coming into my life," Sarah admitted.

"Yep. I was one of the cops who found her and the girls locked in that bedroom. We've gotten pretty close since then."

"Speaking of friends, we just missed Tanner Collins, another friend of mine I was hoping to introduce both of you to. I saw his Lexus leaving the parking lot as we were driving in."

Mitch recognized a hint of disappointment.

"That's too bad. Maybe I'll catch him another time."

～

Tanner pulled the pillow over his head, trying to block out the sound of his neighbors. As per their usual date night routine, they came in amidst an argument that lasted the better part of an hour. As soon as it broke, he knew what to expect. Sure enough, a few minutes of quiet led to what he knew would be a no holds barred, all night bout of 'I don't give a rat's ass who hears us' make up sex.

On a good night, he found it slightly amusing.

Tonight was not one of those nights. Every time he closed his eyes an image of Sarah had appeared. It wasn't any easier, knowing he had about zero percent chance in hell of being a part of her life.

He rolled out of bed and jerked on a pair of jeans over his boxer briefs, deciding to keep the navy blue tee shirt he already wore. He slid on a pair of socks and jammed his feet into his size eleven boots, trying to block out the crescendo of moans and banging headboard. He grabbed wallet and keys, knowing two things, for certain. First, it would only get louder and much more vocal; and second, in his current mood, he just might do something that'd get him thrown out of the condo if he didn't get the hell out of there.

After splashing water on his face, his gaze landed on the card that diner waitress had given him. He picked it up and read it again, stuffing it into his wallet before heading to his car.

◆◆◆

If the annoying thud of overly heavy bass, combined with the stench of cigarette smoke, was any indication of how his night would go, Tanner figured he was in for a big letdown. Instead of using good sense and ditching the plan, Tanner decided anything was an improvement over an entire night of a banshee wailing 'Give it to me, Big Daddy' and the answering grunts of "Take it aaa-ll, Baby…' and 'Tell Big Daddy what you need!'.

"Ah hell…What've I got to lose?" he mumbled, fighting his way through a gyrating throng of….what? Thirty some-things? Uh uh…twenty some-things…some just barely, from the looks of it. He stopped long enough to observe his surroundings. *You're not really gonna do this, are you, Collins?*

He took a deep breath and decided to go for it, pushing his way easily through the throng to end up at the overflowing bar area. Almost immediately, he spotted her, wearing a piece of black, lacey spandex with several strategically placed rips that probably passed for a dress to anyone in *this* place. She balanced on ridiculously tall heels while sucking down some two-toned pink and blue frozen drink through a straw. She stopped drinking long enough to pull a cherry from the glass with her fingers and pop it in her mouth. The stem protruded from her mouth, resembling an unlit fuse on a stick of dynamite. She licked her over-glossed lips painted the exact same shade of pink as the newly painted streaks in her hair.

'Pink' reached over the bar to pull the bride of Frankenstein close for an open mouthed kiss. Ms. Frankenstein, complete with green and black hair, and wearing even less clothing than the other, pulled back, brandishing the cherry stem in her own mouth. Obviously, *this* was the bestie bartender of her reference.

Tanner groaned, more repulsed than he ever thought he could be from a 'girl on girl' scenario. He turned, giving his head a violent shake as he imagined the STD's running rampant in the bar room. He pivoted, fighting his way back to the exit to emerge into the clean night air of downtown Lake Coburn. He glanced north, seeing the tastefully lit sign touting Red McAllister's club. It was located on the opposite side of the street and further down the block, nearer to where he'd parked his car. He knew there'd be either a country band or a good DJ and no smoking, with clientele who acted a little less...daring? Yeah, as much as he hated to admit it, he was definitely getting too old to be playing the one-night-stand game with women barely half his age.

He started walking, hoping the distance was far enough to eliminate at least some of the stench from his clothing. Regardless of being casually dressed, and he had to admit to feeling more comfortable in jeans, a plain black, cotton tee shirt, and western boots, he still preferred smelling like Armani over cigs.

Once inside, he made his way to the bar and smiled at the pleasantly familiar face greeting him behind the bar.

"Hey Tanner, what can I get for you?"

Her east Texas drawl reminded him of growing up in Houston. "How are you tonight, Meagan?"

"Looks like it's going to be just busy enough to make the night fly by without having to go home and pop an ibuprofen or two afterwards."

"Good. I'll have a Dos Equis Amber, please, with a slice of lime if you have any."

"Of course we do," she said, returning with his beer and a plate of extra lime slices.

"Thanks hon, that'll do," he said, closing his eyes to take a deep draught, and appreciating the combination of smoothness and tang. "God, that's good."

"Coldest beer in town," she said, polishing the already shiny surface area. "Where the heck have you been, all reeking of ashtray? Are you two timing me with another bartender one evening every week?" She gave him a good-natured wink.

He took a second swig then pointed the bottle neck to

her. "Meagan, if you'd been witness to what I just saw, you'd know how serious I am when I say 'I'll never stray from you again'."

"That bad, huh? Where'd you go?"

He used his thumb to point in the direction of the place he'd just come from. "Some dive just down the street and a half block south. It didn't take me more than a minute to realize I was in the wrong place." He lifted the collar of his shirt and sniffed at it. "Just long enough to pick up the stench, obviously."

"Stubby's?" Meagan asked, incredulously. "*You* went to Stubby's? I can't imagine a *younger* you going to a place like that, much less the more mature, elegant Doctor Collins. What the hell made you go there?"

Tanner gave her a casual shrug but chose not to answer.

"Or who?" She shook her head, bubbling with laughter. "You were meeting a girl there, weren't you? Oh, Lord, please tell me you knew better than to drink out of any open containers!"

"Hell, I didn't want to touch a surface much less order a drink. I imagine the use of roofies is pretty rampant in a place like that."

"Oh oh," Meagan said, giving him a wink as her voice dropped an octave in warning. "Don't look now, but I think one of them followed your trail over here."

Tanner lowered his head, praying she was wrong. Unfortunately, the sudden reek of cigarette smoke told him differently.

"I thought that was you," Charley drawled, occupying the stool next to him. "Should I be insulted?"

He looked at her and grinned. "Not at all. It's just not my kind of place."

"Yeah…now that I see you in your street clothes, I guess it isn't. Funny, I didn't take you for the contemporary cowboy type." She took the time to pass a critical eye on his choice of attire.

He took another sip of his beer. "More contemporary

than cowboy. Somebody told me once that jeans and boots would make me seem more approachable. It turned out to be comfortable as hell, so I stuck with the look."

Tanner supposed Charley's pause to stare at his crotch was some kind of vixen-ish attempt to say 'Look at me! I'm a woman of the world!' She obviously thought she was making him feel uncomfortable. Poor kid had no idea how in-over-her-head she was.

"You buy me a drink?" she purred, leaning in to give him a good shot of significant cleavage.

"How old are you, Charley?" He looked away to take another swig of beer.

She ran the nail of one finger along his forearm. "I'm old enough to order my own drink. I'll have a Screaming Orgasm," she told Meagan before turning back to Tanner. "And I'm more than old enough to show *you* a good time."

Meagan's eyes sparkled with mischief an instant before she took a deep breath and yelled, at the top of her lungs.

"One Screaming Orgasm coming right up!"

She winked at a gape mouthed Charley. "It's kind of a game we play here at Red's. Whenever anyone orders one of those silly little drinks, the owner wants us to yell it out, kind of like a promotional thing."

Tanner smothered his laughter, seeing as how Meagan looked every bit as serious as he knew she wasn't.

"You *will* have to show me some ID first."

With one hand perched on her barely covered hip, Charley heaved an overly dramatic sigh. She pulled an ID from a tiny little clutch, also reeking of cigarette smoke and held it out for Meagan to see. "Satisfied?" she whined, like she'd just been asked to pick up someone else's dog doo out of a city park.

"Since you're asking, I've gotta admit it's been awhile," Meagan said, snatching the ID and holding it under a type of flashlight for closer examination. She threw it on the counter with a snort. "It's every bit as fake as those boobs of yours."

"They are *not*!" Charley said, putting both hands up to her breasts.

Meagan gave her a big cheesy grin. "I know, but the license is. Now you get on out of here before I call the cops on you for trying to get *me* in trouble with that pitiful excuse for a fake ID. By the way, that tattoo of yours…" She pointed at the single character inked on the inside of the girl's left wrist. "I lived in Korea for twenty years. I don't know what the loser who stole your money told you, but it's a brand of Korean washing powder."

Charley whipped her ID off of the counter and shot Meagan a look that could shrivel a weak man's testicles. Shoving the card back inside her tiny little purse, she flounced off, uttering expletives and making rude hand gestures all the way to the exit. To add insult to injury, she tried to light up a cigarette before she got to the door, garnering the unwanted attention of at least five people, all of whom yelled at her. The bouncer walked over within seconds and threw her out.

～～

Mitchell heard bits of the incident from the shadows, nursing a coke he'd purchased from the bartender at the opposite end of the club. Wanting to keep his presence a secret from Collins, he'd moved close enough to hear some, though not all of the conversation. Gauging how pissed off that diner waitress was when she left, she hadn't been nearly as entertained by the incident as he had.

When Tanner left the bar a minute later, Mitch waited several seconds before hitting the same exit door. He swore low in his throat at the sight of Collins, his hand on the small of the girl's back, helping her into his silver Lexus.

"Son of a bitch," he groaned, watching the car drive off and turn the corner, out of sight. He didn't need a crystal ball to know what those two would be doing for the rest of the night. He had to admit he was disappointed in Collins for his sister's sake.

He'd always considered himself to be a pretty good judge of a man's character. Even though the man had wasted no time in saying he wasn't good enough for Sarah, Mitch had sensed a trace of honor. Hell, it just proved that even he could be wrong. It also proved one more thing. Collins had spoken with total honesty.

Mitch gave his head a slow shake as he headed back inside, this time to the cute brunette's end of the bar.

"Yes sir, what can I get for you tonight?" She beamed up at him.

He perked up at the twang that had Texas/Louisiana border stamped all over it. "Seven and seven, hold the lemon, one ice cube please," he said. "Uh, Miss?" he asked, pulling out his wallet when she turned away to prepare it.

"Yes?"

He took out his driver's license and handed it to her. "Don't you need to check this first? I may be underage and trying to pass off a fake ID."

She cracked a huge, good-natured grin. "Heard all that, did ya?"

"I didn't catch it all, but I admit I was trying to. How'd you know her ID was a fake? You got an infrared moonbeam back here or something?"

She broke into laughter as she pulled out the bottle of Seagram's whiskey and a glass and started to pour. "I didn't *know* for sure, but I had a hunch. I bluffed and she took the bait." She shook her head as she added the soda and ice. "That poor girl was more worried that I thought her…ahem …*cleavage*…was fake." She put her hands up to her own comparatively modest neckline, and mimicked the look the young girl had given her. "They are *not*!"

Mitch leaned forward. "Tell me the truth, what did her tattoo read?"

"Your guess is as good as mine. I've never been to Korea in my life."

Mitch put his head back and bellowed with laughter. "That's pretty good. I guess you get used to that sort of thing, working as a bartender. You been doing this long?"

She made a face. "Long enough, and believe me, in

some joints a lot worse than this place."

He made it a point to look around again, as though he hadn't already given it the once over from force of habit. "It's a nice place, my first time here."

"Really? Well, welcome to Red's!" She placed his drink in front of him. "The first one's free, but it'll be two-fifty after that."

"You got some kind of special going on for new customers?" he asked, thinking he'd paid more than two-fifty for a drink ten years ago.

"Only for military. First one's on the house and the rest are half price. Red says we should show our thanks and respect to our service men and women."

"Did I say something to make you think I'm in the service?"

She leaned over, resting both arms on the bar. "You didn't have to." She winked at him before walking away to tend to another customer.

Before long, she returned. "You ready for another one?"

"You sure there's no limit?"

"Not unless you start getting too big for your britches, in which case, I'll have to either cut you off or throw you out."

"Fair enough," he said.

"You back for good?"

"Nah, I'm down visiting some family. Tell me the truth. How'd you know I was military? It's been a while since my last high and tight. Surely it's grown out enough not to give me away."

She gave him a sad smile. "My fiancé was a Marine. He carried himself a certain way...so straight, proud...you move like him."

"Was?" he asked, dreading her answer. He'd seen that look too many times.

She nodded. "IED in a place called Now Zad Valley in some province I can never remember the name of in southern Afghanistan."

"Helmand province," he finished for her as she nodded. "When?"

"December of '09...just passed the third anniversary. Marine recon unit Task Force Raider."

"Apocalypse Now-Zad..."

Her head cocked curiously. "Christopher used to call it that too. Were you a Raider?" she asked, sounding hopeful.

"No, I'm sorry, but I am a jarhead. The 1st Recon Battalion."

"Oooo...Black Diamond." Her brows raised in obvious admiration. "Sons of Satan..."

"Oorah! You know your military divisions."

"Only the Marines." She smiled, wiping at a corner of her eye. "I don't know what kind of a Marine he was, but Chris was a hell of a good man. Three years already," she mused. "If you'd asked me then, I never would have said I'd have survived for this long without him." She sighed and wiped up a condensation spot from the bar. "But, here I am. Still serving drinks."

"Life goes on, even after you bury a Marine."

"Yes...yes, it certainly does."

He sipped slowly at his drink. "So, how long have you worked here?"

"Since the place opened a couple of years ago. I worked in another of his clubs in Lafayette until it burned down. When he opened this place in Lake Coburn, he gave his old employees first choice. I decided to make the move along with him."

He leaned forward in his chair. "Where'd you live before then? No way in hell did you get that accent in Lafayette, the heart of Acadiana and Cajun Country."

She smiled, shaking her head. "A little town in central east Texas with a population of 99, even though the sign still says 100. Trust me, you would never have heard of it...unless you were born there, like I was."

"Thousands of towns like that all over this country. There's no shame in being from one."

"I'm not the one ashamed." She shrugged at the question in his gaze. "I guess I've always enjoyed raising a few eyebrows with my actions."

"A real trouble maker, huh?"

She leaned forward. "Oh yeah, a sinner of the worst kind."

"What kind is that?"

She grabbed a towel, twisting it into a tight knot. "Unrepentant."

"He slapped the bar with one hand. "Shameless!"

"Exactly…and Lord a mercy, if they knew I worked in a bar, I'd be written out of the town registry forever."

"Undoubtedly. Hell, I bet they'd even change that population sign…get it down to double digits again."

"You may be right," she drawled, then started laughing. "Working in a bar is not something I see myself doing for the rest of my life, but for now, it's convenient. Red pays well, provides me with an insurance plan, and I wanted the smoke-free environment. He's the best boss I've ever had."

Mitch scanned the spacious club and nodded. "It is nice to be able to breathe in here. You got allergies or something?"

"Something," she said, letting him know she didn't appreciate the questions.

"Message received, loud and clear, Ma'am," he said. "That guy that just left, the one Miss Generation X was all over, is he a friend of yours?"

She gave him a shrug. "I know him because he comes in here every now and then. He's an old friend of my boss and his wife's, I believe."

"Know anything else about him?"

"Other than he seems to be a nice enough guy, no. *I* make it a point not to gossip about people."

"Are you saying other people gossip about him?"

Her eyes flashed in warning. "I'm saying it's none of my business what the guy does as long as he pays for his drinks and stays out of trouble, which he does. Tanner's never rude to me and he's a decent tipper. Do you need anything else?"

The tone of her voice let him know the subject of Tanner Collins was good and closed. "No ma'am, that'll be all for me tonight." He downed the last of his drink and got up to leave. He'd taken two steps toward the door when she called out to him.

"Hey, Marine!"

He turned to face her. "Ma'am?".

"You take care of yourself out there, you hear me? And uh, Semper Fi."

"Oorah...Ma'am."

Chapter 6

"So, are you leaning one way or the other concerning your career, Mitch?" Sarah asked, trying not to sound hopeful. As badly as she wanted him to retire, she knew he'd have to come to his own decision in his own time.

"Not yet," he said, scraping carrots from Danni's chin to shovel it back into her mouth. "There you go, baby girl. And your momma was afraid I couldn't handle this." He turned toward Sarah, pointing a thumb at his chest. "I'm a Marine, sis…I can handle anything they throw at me."

Danni chose that moment to spray her uncle with a fine mist of pureed carrots. Sarah burst into laughter as her big, bad Marine brother jumped up from the chair like he was avoiding sniper fire.

"Just be glad it was only food this time," she snorted, wiping tears of laughter from her eyes before throwing a dampened paper towel at Mitch. "There is nothing quite as humbling as taking care of a toddler."

"Good God! That stuff is just the right viscosity for prime coverage, that's for damn sure. He wiped off his shirt then leaned over to address the culprit. "Danni girl, with that excellent aim of yours, I believe you've got a future as a Marine."

Sarah pulled a disposable wipe from its container and cleaned the carrots from her daughter's chin. "Let's get her through teething, walking, and potty training before we plan her military career, shall we? Besides, she'll never want to be that far from her mommy, will you sweetie-pie?" she gushed, as the toddler squealed with delight.

Mitch leaned closer to his niece, who reached out with chubby fingers to pat his cheeks. "I guess you're right, but it'll definitely be the Marine's loss." He grabbed her sticky fingers and put them in his mouth, making her shriek with laughter.

"Blech!" He pulled back, wiping his mouth with a napkin. "That stuff is foul."

"It's just carrots, Mitch. If it tastes foul it's probably from the other stuff on her hands. You know, like drool, snot, spit-up…boogers…" She laughed again as Mitch ran to the sink to wash out his mouth.

"Gah! You could have warned me!" he sputtered.

"I figured you were old enough to know not to stick her fingers in your mouth, at least without washing them first. She's a toddler for chrissakes…what else would she do in her spare time? Target practice?"

"I hope not," he said, lifting Danni from her high chair. "I can't imagine her aim being any better than it already—" His features suddenly scrunched in distaste. "I'm detecting some type of noxious gas release."

"That may be more than gas, Uncle Mitch."

He stuck his face near her bottom and jerked back, gagging. "Good Lord! That *can't* all be coming from her!"

"Come on, macho man…even Tanner Collins didn't get freaked out that badly," she said, smiling as she remembered an incident a couple of months earlier when he'd been holding one of the babies during a massive release of poo. "He took it like a champ compared to you."

"Yeah, well I bet he hadn't recently been sprayed with pureed carrots, and tasted…God knows what! All this is— Man this is overkill."

"You want to change her diaper for me? It'll be good practice for when you settle down and have a baby of your own one day." Her brother's face turned a shade paler, tinted with a faint green hue.

∾

Mitch recovered quickly enough to know she was setting him up. "That particular task is way beyond my pay grade. It calls for an immediate transfer of duties to her mama." He swiveled his upper body, trying to hold his breath until Sarah had taken the foul smelling package off his hands to carry her to the nursery. He collected Sammi from her high chair and followed his sister into the room. "That can't all be from carrots," he said, immediately regretting the quick peek over Sarah's shoulder.

"That's vegetable beef from supper last night."

He carried Sammi to the far corner of the room to get some fresh air. "You might want to strike that from their list of grub from now on. That can't be normal."

"They eat a variety of foods, I assure you, all producing pretty much the same results. I haven't had much experience with other babies, but from what I've witnessed, all babies stink the same, Uncle Mitch."

She turned toward him, holding out the freshly diapered child. "Here—trade with me so I can change Sammi's diaper, too. Clean her up while you're at it, *if* you think you can handle it."

He took the much improved and diapered Danni from her, grabbing a pack of pleasantly scented wipes. "Now *these* I can handle." He lay his niece on one of two changing tables and pulled out a few wipes while starting up a one sided dialog with her. "You see, little lady—back in the sandbox—what you civilians call the middle east—we don't have a lot of fresh water to bathe in. So we pull out the old reliable wipes for a GI shower. It's not as good as a real shower but a couple dozen of these'll get the grit out for a little bit." Danni screeched when he pinched her nose with the cloth to clean it. "Check your fire, sweet-cheeks! You got some leftover grub in your snot locker." A couple more passes with the wipes, and his niece looked and smelled presentable again. "Now...all scrubbed up and good to go."

He glanced over at his sister, deciding it was as good a time as any to get a reading on a particular situation. "I'd like to see Collins top that. Speaking of him, I saw him at Red's club last night." He watched her for any tell-tale signs of interest. As he'd suspected, the barest hint of a flush appeared on her cheeks while her head craned with irrefutable interest.

"You met Tanner?"

"I actually met him at the farmer's market that day you and I went. After you went to the car, he and I exchanged a few words. Last night I was at Red's and he showed up. We didn't talk though."

Sarah sat in one rocker with Sammi, while pointing at the other for her brother to sit.

Mitch sat and, following his sister's example, positioned Danni on his left shoulder to start up a rhythmic patting on her diapered bottom. "I think it'd be a mistake for you to expect anything other than friendship from him, sis. It's not that I don't think he's a nice guy."

"What makes you think I'm interested in him?"

"He's the type that comes by it so easily it turns into more of a habit for him than anything else."

"Why do you think I'm interested in Tanner?"

"It doesn't mean he's a bad guy, just not used to turning it dow—"

"Mitch!"

He jerked around at her sharply barked command.

"I'm *not* interested in him."

Mitch gave her a casual shrug. "Okay."

"Why would you think that? Did he say anything?"

"No...but I know what I see in your face and hear in your tone when someone mentions his name."

"I'm no—"

He lifted his hand, cutting off the rest of her comment. "He's trouble for you, sis. That's all I'm saying. Don't talk anymore...this one's almost out."

After another five minutes of rocking and patting bottoms, Mitchell rose from the chair and quietly made his way to the crib with Danni's name stenciled on one side with pink and green lettering. He laid her gingerly on the mattress and covered her with the quilt, patting her bottom until he thought she'd stay sleeping. When it looked as though Sarah was ready to follow suit, he took the opportunity to slip out, leaving the house long before his sister could fire any more rounds of questions at him.

∾

"Did you see Mitch?" Sarah asked, entering the kitchen.

Leah pulled a large pack of chicken breast out of the fridge and placed it in the sink. "Just long enough to see him hit the door like someone had set his tail on fire. What are you after him for?"

"Information…dammit!" Sarah swore as she opened the door in time to see the trail of dust her brother had left in the driveway with his rental.

"What's going on?" Leah asked, reaching for a well-worn cookbook on the shelf.

"It's nothing." Sarah grabbed a glass and poured herself some filtered water. She drank, remembering the latest of several dreams she'd had. All steamy enough to liquefy butter…every one of them had left her shaky and wanting after awakening. Each dream episode had involved the *one* man she knew she had a snowball's chance in hell of attracting…Tanner Collins. She blushed, thinking about the latest one, erotic enough to make her awake drenched with the moist heat of her own desire. Totally unsatisfying as well, since Sammi had awakened her, crying for a bottle.

She hadn't told a soul about her dreams, thought she'd done a damn good job of disguising her emotions when anyone mentioned his name. Or not, considering her brother had picked up on something. Mitchell had never been very good at catching subtle hints in his civilian life prior to the Marines. Either she sucked at concealing her feelings, or her brother's military experience had enabled him to sense what no one else had been able to.

Good God, let that be the case.

She'd die if anyone else suspected what Mitch did, especially Tanner.

∼◡∽

"Look at these two munchkins! They must have grown six inches since I saw them last."

Sarah beamed at Melanie, who spun around, holding a giggling Sammi. "They like to eat, and no matter what I feed them for supper, they still wake up for their two a.m.

bottles…little piglets."

"Mmm…adorable little piglets," Melanie crooned, kissing Sammi on the belly. "Oh, I hope when I have kids one day they'll be this cute."

"Please—with your genetics, they're bound to be gorgeous."

"I think the father will have some say in the situation."

"I'm predicting your DNA will dominate. But speaking of perspective fathers, you heard from Liam Nash lately?" Sarah asked.

"Not for a couple of months now." Mel took a deep breath and released it slowly. "Not since Angelique Baptiste broke his heart by choosing Mike Harper over him."

"I don't think he was all that heart-broken by it, just mildly disappointed. Trust me, he'll get over it, and when he does—"

"What?" Mel cut in. "He'll come running back to a mouthy red-head, with big boobs and a wide butt? Yeah, I'm sure girls like me are right up there at the top of *Mr. so-fine-he-could-have-his-own-calendar*'s list of perfect women."

Sarah dabbed at some drool on the front of her shirt with a baby wipe. "Oh stop. You have a great figure, and don't forget that you have law enforcement in common, and I'm sure the fact that you're a technological genius is a big plus."

"I can talk cops and robbers with him for sure, but I doubt Liam's impressed much by my computer skills."

"Well, you and my big brother have that in common for sure, and I know for a fact he likes boobs and redheads."

Mel pursed her lips. "I can't argue with the fact that your big bro is a hottie. I've never seen an active Marine who wasn't in shape, but Mitchell seems especially…fit."

Sarah's heart soared with hopefulness. She and Melanie were already best friends, and Danni and Sammi both adored their 'Aunt Mel'. Wouldn't it be that much more wonderful to have her as a sister-in-law, an official member of the family?

"But I didn't come over here for you to set me up with your brother, Sarah."

"I know that, but he's trying to decide whether it's time to re-up or return to civilian life. I'm not gonna lie, I want him out of the military and maybe him finding a girl *here* would do the trick. If that girl turned out to be some bodacious redhead I just happen to know, well that wouldn't break my heart a bit." Sarah jumped at the sound of someone clearing his throat behind her. She spun on her heels to see her brother standing with his arms crossed and wearing an amused expression.

"I just got home and you're trying to marry me off already?"

"I know, right?" Mel said, stepping up beside him to stare down at Sarah. "I was about to ask her if she'd planned the wedding yet."

Sarah narrowed her eyes at her brother and friend. "I can't help it if I want to see you home in one piece, Mitch. It stinks having to worry about you over in the Middle East." She stopped to sniff the air. "Speaking of stink...pew, Danni." She wrinkled her nose at the distinct aroma of 'eau de dirty diaper'. Heading for the nursery, she threw them an over-the-shoulder comment. "By the way, you two would make gorgeous babies."

∿

Mitch joined in with Melanie's laughter as he turned to the attractive red head. "She is some kinda pushy, ain't she?"

Mel adjusted Sammi on her hip. "Not very subtle, that's for damn sure. Wants *you* married off...quick."

He stared after his departed sister. "Last time I saw her she wasn't nearly as outspoken. I guess she couldn't speak her mind the entire time she was married to that psychotic shit brick. Now she makes sure her opinion is heard."

"There's nothing wrong with that. It just means she's healing."

He nodded emphatically. "One of several things I agree with you on, so far. I suppose that's why she's trying to shove us together. But—"

"You are in no way ready for that, and I'm actually kind of hung up on someone else, so maybe one of us should tell her to stop?"

"Officer Finley, you and I really do think alike. How serious is that hang up?" he said, giving her a wink, then smiled at the low, rather sexy chuckle she emitted.

"A little more on my part since I doubt he knows I exist."

"Has he met you?"

"Oh, yeah, a few times," she admitted.

"Trust me, Mel, he *knows* you exist. You're not the kind of girl a guy meets and doesn't notice."

Her head tilted slightly. "You think so, huh. I guess that's a good thing."

"It's a very good thing. So, even though we aren't destined for marriage, maybe you could show me around this town? Catch a couple of flicks, and do some dancing?"

"I'm not from this area, so I don't know much about places in Lake Coburn, other than Red's place. I've lived in the Lafayette area since my early teens and since becoming a cop, have worked and lived there, exclusively."

"I don't mind doing a little driving."

"That's good, because I'd suggest Mulate's in Breaux Bridge for some good Cajun dancing. For country, you can't get any better than Red's right here in Lake Coburn. I got a room at the Marriott about a block from his club tonight. His house band is kick ass, and if I drink too much I can walk to the hotel." Her face suddenly lit up. "I bet I can get us tickets to the Trace Adkins concert at the Casino the first weekend of next month. Will you still be in for that?"

"I leave on the second to go back," he said, shaking his head regretfully. "But, you've got me until then, pretty girl." Mitch smiled as he witnessed the slightest blushing of her cheeks. It just proved that even though she was a cop, Mel was still a woman.

"Awe...thanks, Mitch. You are so sweet."

"And I'm not saying that just hoping to get lucky, either. Believe it or not, I'm not that much into casual sex."

"That's too bad," she said, her brow scrunched as she clucked her tongue. "And here I was about to ask you for an afternoon of that very thing."

He laughed. "Yeah, sure you were."

She set Sammi in the center of the playpen and straightened before shrugging a shoulder. "Seriously, Mitch, it's been awhile since I've had a real blow-the-carburetor-out round of mind-blowing, nothing but fun *sex* without having to worry about committing to anyone."

Mitchell's spine stiffened, stretched him to his full height of barely six feet. "Really?" He watched her pivot slowly to face him, the tiniest trace of a smile tugging at the corner of her plump bottom lip.

Mel lifted one neatly trimmed nail to his face, drew it gently, slowly down from the top of his upper lip to his chin, settling in the distinctive dent he'd inherited from his father. A barely detectable up and down head movement accompanied her huskily whispered comeback.

"Of course...not."

His body, reacting to her tone, leaned to touch her, even as his mind came to a screeching halt. "Wait...What?" he said, struggling to shift gears, to throw his body into reverse in order to stop its forward progress. He saw it then, the slight lift of her left brow before her abrupt burst into laughter.

She didn't even attempt to quell her resulting snorts of laughter as she mocked him. "Not that much into casual sex, my *ass!*"

He nodded, and closed the gap between them, his attitude far from acceptance of the situation. Her hoots of laughter continued, head thrown back, eyes streaming with tears. By the time she gained some semblance of control over her gasps of laughter, he was in her face, and ready to drive his point home.

With one hand clasped firmly at the back of her neck, he tugged her close, clamping his mouth over hers and cutting her breath. After a moment of hard, desperate grinding, he gentled the kiss, nipping, tasting, pulling her lower lip into his mouth, wanting her to recognize she was in over her head, to accept defeat at the hands of his superior skills.

But Mel, herself a worthy adversary, had other ideas, as well as a skillset of her own. She took it to an entirely different level...biting, savoring, sucking hard at his tongue, her fingers threading through his hair. Obviously, playtime wasn't over until *she* gave the signal.

As a result, what began simply as a way to shut her up, turned into a heated, vertical, hard bodies and straining limbs...hands pulling, tugging, reaching out for an even closer physical connection, clothes withstanding.

He couldn't tell who conceded first. Maybe they had at exactly the same time, but the contact ended abruptly, leaving them both flushed and heated with lustful longing.

A little off balance, Mel staggered slightly before correcting her stance. She exhaled and cleared her throat gently. "Not bad, Sergeant Hebert, not bad at all."

He grinned, and still somewhat determined to dominate, reached out with his right hand to lightly drag his forefinger from her jawline down her neck to the throbbing pulse at the base of her throat.

"That's *Master* Sergeant, and don't you forget it, Officer Finley."

In hindsight, he should have known better. A sudden and distinct pressure of her hand squeezing his balls had him sucking in air and tensing. She pursed her slightly swollen lips and arched delicate red brows over eyes that sparkled with mischief.

"That's *Detective* Finley, and don't *you* forget it."

Chapter 7

Tanner approached the entrance of Red's club, wondering if it was possible for anything to pull him out of his current rut of boredom. He tugged open the heavy door, his body and mind responding immediately to the telltale rhythm and bass of the house band. He paid the entrance fee to have his hand stamped, and stood for a minute searching for familiar faces in the crowd. He caught sight of Red behind the bar, passing a customer a beer then stopping to address one of his employees.

It was funny how things had turned out for the two of them. Considering their history of bad blood during the college years at LSU, not to mention the fact that Tiffany had left him for Red, he was continually amazed that they'd since become such good friends.

He approached the bar, catching Red's eye, and held out his hand.

Red sent his bouncer off with a final pat to his arm before grabbing hold of Tanner's hand. "Hey, buddy. You look like you could use a beer." He reached inside the cooler and pulled out an icy bottle, popped the top and handed it over.

Tanner took a generous swig and wiped his mouth, smiling at the cold welcome goodness of his favorite brew. "Thanks man, I needed that after today."

"Rough day at the hospital?"

"Not so much the hospital, but a rough day, none the less."

"Aw...that's either woman problems or family problems or both, for the unfortunate few. Which is it?" Red asked, wearing a knowing grin.

"Family," he lied—or rather, told a partial truth. Any day he couldn't keep thoughts of Sarah from invading his pitifully love-addled brain, inevitably turned into a bad day. He'd woken up with her on his mind, the scent of her carrying over from a dream that left him throbbing with need for her. It had been decades since he'd had to revert to cold showers over a phone call to someone ready and willing to fulfill his needs. He shivered, remembering the shock of frigid water on his hot skin in this morning's shower. Even then, it had taken awhile to suppress his physical need.

Before he'd finished his first cup of coffee, his mother's disturbing phone call came in, tipping the scales of his tolerance to a dangerous level.

"My dad needs heart surgery, and no matter how much I tell my mother I *don't do hearts*, she insists that I do the procedure." He chuckled at Red's puzzled expression. "I know, right? She's probably afraid the top heart specialist in Houston will somehow contaminate dad's blue blood."

Red shook his head and barked out a laugh. "Man, no wonder you were such a pompous asshole in college!"

Tanner nodded sadly. "Sorry, bro. I came by it honestly. It wasn't until they insulted Angelique that it hit me how badly they'd influenced my opinions."

Red came around the bar to stand next to him. "I doubt you could help it, and if it's any consolation, you're only about half the asshole you used to be."

Tanner slapped his hand over his own heart. "Thanks man! That means a lot coming from a white trash club owner like you." He joined in on Red's raucous laughter, stopping short when three women approached the bar.

Tiffany McAllister wrapped her hands around Red's bicep. "Here you are," she crooned. "Hi Tanner, but I'm stealing my hubby for a dance." Red took his wife's hand and grinned, letting her pull him out to the floor.

Sarah's voice caught Red's attention. "Hey Tanner, have you met Melanie Finley yet? She's spending the night in town to get her fill of the house band."

Tanner forced himself to pull his gaze from Sarah's

sweet lips long enough to take notice of the busty redhead standing beside her. "I don't think I've had the pleasure yet. It's nice to meet you Melanie."

"It's nice to meet you too, Tanner. But call me Mel, please. Everyone else does," she said.

"Mel…" The pieces fell into place. "You're *Officer* Mel?"

"That's *Detective* Finley, she's been promoted recently," a male voice added. Mitchell stepped up carrying three beers. He gave Mel and Sarah each one, while keeping the last for himself. "Tanner, isn't it?" he said, looking a tad smug.

Tanner nodded, as he took the other man's hand in a strong grip. "Mitchell, right?" He couldn't help but notice Sarah's look of bewilderment.

"You two know each other?"

"We've met, Sis."

"Briefly," Tanner added before turning back to Sarah. "How've you been? Are the girls okay?"

"Sis, you ready for that dance?" Mitch said, sounding a little too insistent.

"Next time, maybe," Sarah said, smiling up at her brother.

"You heard her, *Master* Sergeant," Melanie said, grabbing hold of Mitchell's arm and pushing him toward the dance floor. "Let's see if you can two-step as well as you can jitterbug."

Tanner focused on Sarah's smile as she watched Mitch and Melanie join throng of dancers. Eventually her gaze returned to his.

"To answer your question, the girls and I are fine."

"Good! That's what I wanted to hear. They cut anymore teeth lately?"

"Yeah, a couple more last week, and Sammi has another one about to break through, I think. It keeps them both a little on the cranky side."

"And mom too, maybe?" he said.

"I don't have much reason to be cranky. We're safe

and cared for, and I've got so much help from Leah and Daniel."

"They care about you and the girls. Anyone can see that."

She cupped her hand to her ear. "What's that?" she said, raising her voice over the driving beat of music.

Before he could repeat it, she put up her hand to stop him.

"Follow me!" she said, pulling him behind her.

Like a leash-trained pup, he followed, head up, and obedient. He allowed himself a few moments to bask happily in her presence before busting his own bubble. *Down, boy...she deserves better than you.*

They reached a table in the corner and he pulled out her chair before seating himself directly across from her

"This is much better," she said, settling into her spot.

With the strain of trying to catch every word she spoke removed from the equation, Tanner found it much easier to concentrate on the sight before him. She gathered her locks in one hand and lifted them while using the other to fan her neck. The subtle scent of her perfume, delicious and sexy as hell, drove home a pure and simple fact. He truly was a glutton for punishment.

"Now, what was it you said?"

He sat there, stupefied with wanting her and finally managed to shake himself into some type of awareness. "Uh...I think I'd said that it was easy to see how much the LeBlancs care for you and the twins."

She gave him an enthusiastic nod. "They're the best. Daniel refuses to let me pay for a thing the girls and I need—he insists that I put all my money in savings. I keep telling them both that I've got plenty enough put aside, and enough coming in to be out on my own. They keep begging me to stay."

"What do you want to do?" he asked.

"Well, don't get me wrong, I appreciate the extra hands. It's not easy raising twins alone, believe me. But, it's *nothing* compared to trying to raise them with a husband who beat the hell out of me." She took a sip of her beer and stared thoughtfully at the label. "It would be a first for me, you know? My own place, just me and my girls…"

"Mistress of your own domain," he said.

She looked up at him, her face registering surprise at his contribution. "That's right; it's not so much to be out on my own, but, I guess I…" She faltered, as though searching for the right words.

"You just need to know that you can," he added, knowing he'd hit pay dirt when her face lit up.

"Exactly! It's…it's important to me."

"I get that."

"Do you?" she said, the creases in her forehead registering her doubt.

"Sure. As a parent, you need to know that you can provide for them."

"I do, and I want them to grow up thinking they can do the same thing if push comes to shove and they ever have to. I mean, in a perfect world, they'd be able to count on their husbands for positive support. But, sometimes the world isn't that perfect."

"It will be for them, Sarah," he said, thinking he'd gladly be first in line to beat the hell out of any man who mistreated one of those girls…grown up or otherwise.

"Well, I'd be grateful for that." She sipped from her beer and lowered it to the table.

"How's the job treating you?" Again, her face lit up, revealing how much she must like her job.

"I *love* my job. I adore the medical personnel. Dr. Maze is a dream of a boss, and the nurses and technicians, even the office personnel. Everyone is so close. The work has been so gratifying for me. I mean they do lose patients, sometimes. Just before Angelique left, they lost one of the long-term radiation patients, an elderly woman. I didn't get to meet her, but everyone was pretty torn up about it. Just this week we completed radiation treatments on three different patients, with excellent final prognoses to remain cancer free. I've never had a job that was so fulfilling before. She gave her bottle of couple of spins. "I have to admit though, losing both my parents the way I did, I could see how a patient's death would make it difficult to go to work some days."

She sipped from her beer then turned her attention back to him. "How about you, Tanner? Has anything interesting happened with you lately?" She tapped her chin with her fingers. "Um, something along the lines of saving a room full of people from an addict waving a gun?"

He grimaced and sucked in his breath. "You heard about that?"

"Of course I did, everyone heard about it."

"But we work out of different departments, and I didn't think—"

"Oh, come on Dr. Collins! Hospitals have direct lines at light speed as far as gossip is concerned; you ought to know *that* by now."

"Well, I do know our PR department tried like hell to keep it out of the news. Camera crews disrupting the ER and so forth, so we do what we can to keep things quiet."

"I'm guessing you didn't see it on You Tube?"

He stared, dumbfounded at her dimpled grin. "God, please tell me you're joking."

Her eyes sparkled with laughter. "I am, but it's only because it was a slow night. It would have been a different story if there had been a full moon."

He allowed himself a moment to be thankful the incident *hadn't* been plastered all over You Tube and Facebook. "You're probably right." He rubbed at the back of his neck, trying to ease the kink of tension he'd suddenly developed. A male voice cut in from behind him.

"What's she right about this time?" Mitch said, pulling out a chair for Melanie and sitting beside her.

"I was just telling Tanner he needed to come by and see how much the twins have grown since he's seen them last."

He threw her a look of gratitude. "I've got the next

couple of days to myself. Maybe I'll do that."

"I certainly wish you'd try." Her gaze brimmed with warmth and sincerity.

He nodded, jumping slightly at the sound of his cellphone ringing and vibrating in his pocket. He scanned the screen, groaning as his mother's name appeared. "Oh hell, I gotta take this. Excuse me, please." He pushed up from the table to stand a few feet away.

He answered it, steeling himself for bad news. "Mother, has something happened?"

∾

Sarah only tore her gaze from Tanner when someone nudged her in the side.

"What's going on?"

She turned to Tiffany. "I don't know. He got a phone call, and it's upset him, I think. I hope nothing's wrong."

He ended his call and returned to the table. "I have to head to Houston. My father's had a heart attack."

Tiffany gasped as Sarah raised her hand to her mouth. "Oh, Tanner," she breathed. "Did he…is it serious?"

"He's stabilized for now, but his surgery will be scheduled as soon as they think he's strong enough. What began as stints has blossomed into a bypass surgery— possibly a double, depending on test results."

"Oh, I'm so sorry," Sarah groaned, wishing she could do something to help. "I'll say a prayer for him."

He looked at her suddenly, as though the concept was new to him. "I'd appreciate that. Thank you, Sarah."

"Tanner, do you need me to call the hospital for you?" Tiffany asked.

"I'll call Dr. Hanson when I'm on the road, Tiff. I'm off for the next two days so they'll have time to find someone to fill in. I need to stop by my apartment to pick up a few things. I may be gone longer than a couple of days. So…I guess I'll see y'all when I see y'all." He gave them a half wave and headed for the exit.

Sarah stood watching as he slowly wove his way through the crowd, catching glimpses of his blond hair while Tiffany rambled on beside her.

"Poor guy, I hope he's okay for the drive. His dad is just over sixty. I wonder if Tanner's had his heart checked out recent…Hey, where are you going?"

"I'll be right back!" Sarah shouted to Tiffany just before immersing herself in the thickening crowd. She scooted and barreled and 'Excuse me'd' her way through the throng of dancers and browsers to finally make it to the exit, only to find no Tanner. She barged through the door and searched the immediate parking area, with no sign of him.

"Oh damn! Double damn!" she swore, disappointed to her core at missing him. Despondent and suddenly wanting nothing more than to go home, she swiveled and yanked on the door. It flew open, nearly sending her flying along with it.

"Tanner!" she said, staring up at the shadowed features of his chiseled face.

"Hey, didn't I just leave you back there?" he asked, pointing over his shoulder.

"Yeah…Yes, you did, but…I…" she stammered before pausing to get her thoughts together as he stepped out, letting the door shut behind him.

"Sarah?"

Her name seemed to reverberate in the sudden relative silence—his voice deep, resonating, and so damn sexy it gave her chills. Suddenly, she felt as inept as a silly, young teenager, pining over her first puppy love. "Nothing…it's…nothing." She spun toward the door, but his hand on her wrist stopped her.

"What is it, Sarah?"

She couldn't have walked away from that voice if she'd wanted to. She turned to face him again, bracing herself for the perfection of his facial features, this time awash with the club entrances overhead lighting. No amount of bracing could prepare her for the tenderness in those blue eyes. She took a deep breath, releasing it slowly.

"You…looked…like you needed a hug, that's all."

His reaction was immediate, and so very touching. Tanner's smile, genuine and heartfelt, immediately transformed his handsome face into something more along the lines of absolutely adorable.

"I did?"

Sarah stared up at him, and at some point, realized her head was bobbing up and down like the bobble head of a dash ornament, only in slow motion. She stopped abruptly. "You definitely did."

"Well?"

"What?" She twisted her hands, uncertain about what her next move should be.

He opened his arms wide. "It'd be a damn shame for you to come all the way out here and not follow through."

She stepped forward, welcoming his embrace as she wrapped her arms tightly around his waist. "I'm sorry about your father, Tanner. Please drive safely."

"I will," he said, releasing her. "And thank you."

She stepped back, nodding. "You're welcome. I hope everything turns out okay." Absolutely certain she'd made a complete ass of herself, she swiveled, and headed back inside, choosing not to respond to his rushed, "Thanks again."

Chapter 8

He'd been driving for two hours, and he still couldn't get her out of his mind. In minutes, he'd be arriving at the Houston Heart Institute, and he could still feel her arms around his waist. No matter how many times he talked himself out of thinking about her for whatever reasons: she deserved better, or he'd never wanted children, or he was fooling himself if he thought he could ever change, her image always managed to infuse his mind. Sarah, with the babies, or dancing with him, or grinning up at him...he couldn't shake it. The voice of the genie in the GPS sliced through his thoughts.

"Turn right at light then take immediate left."

He did what his phone's GPS told him to do.

"Arriving at destination on right."

Navigational systems were a wonderful thing. If only they'd create one to keep him from screwing up.

*"Do **not** take next left to the club named Stubby's. Bear right at next intersection to avoid picking up sales woman at the Baby Boutique. Avoid impending one-night-stand with busty brunette in the lab. Do not piss off girl of your dream's only sibling...especially if said sibling is a U.S. Marine."*

He pulled his car into a parking spot relatively near the correct entrance of the huge hospital. The place was massive, as was everything in Houston in comparison to Lake Coburn. It was near the top as far as heart health care was concerned. No doubt they had the best technical equipment money could buy. As much as he envied that particular perk he also knew the disadvantages of working and living in a city like Houston; one being rush hour traffic.

He got out of his car and took several seconds to

stretch, working the kinks out of his back before heading to the entrance. It took a full ten minutes to find his father's correct wing and room. Visiting hours were over, but his father's condition was serious enough for them to let immediate family members through.

After a soft rap on the door, Tanner entered the spacious suite. He paused for a moment, trying to digest the sight of his father, his face as gray as an overcast sky protruding from a sea of white sheets.

As accustomed as he was to seeing his patients in that condition on a daily basis, the sight of Justin Collins shocked him into a brief silence. His father, normally the picture of health and vigor, lay there, still as death, eyes closed, with a plethora of electronic leads and plastic tubing trailing from his limbs to hang limply from the bed. The heart monitor beeped steadily, a relief no doubt for his mother, who occupied the chair pulled up next to the bed. Her head tilted back onto the floral cushion, eyes closed with mouth slightly opened. Her right elbow rested on the bedrail, as her hand clutched her husband's.

Tanner swiped at his face, barely finding the breath to whisper a single word at the sight of them.

"Jesus."

Neither of them budged, and he took several tentative steps forward, close enough to see the lines of worry and exhaustion on his mother's face. He found it amazing that, despite their lack of compassion for anyone below their station, they still seemed to love each other.

He approached, touched his mother lightly on the shoulder.

"Mother," he whispered.

Celine's eyelashes fluttered, she opened her eyes and lifted her head, wincing at some obvious stiffness or pain. She tensed as her glance flew from him to her husband, relaxing only when she realized he still slept soundly. She removed her hand from his and stood up, creeping toward the door and motioning for Tanner to follow.

Once in the hallway, she pulled the door closed

quietly behind them. "He had a horrendous night and needs to rest," she said, finally meeting Tanner's gaze. "Thank you for coming, son; It will mean a lot to your father."

"Of course I came," he said. "Did you honestly think I wouldn't?"

"We weren't sure we'd ever see you again…after that last incident," she said, sniffing into one of her ever-present linen hankies she pulled from the pocket of her Chanel jacket.

"You were both out of line—" He stopped, waved a hand to cut off the subject. "That's an entirely different issue and it doesn't matter. What have the doctors said?"

"He's scheduled for surgery in the morning. They wanted to give him a day to recuperate from the attack."

"Do you know if he was given a dose of thrombolystics? They may have called it a clot buster and it would have been administered in a shot form."

"I think so, in the ER maybe?" She rubbed her fingers lightly over her brow.

"Or in the ambulance?"

"Justin wouldn't let me call an ambulance. He said after that broken leg episode he'd never set foot in another one of those things. Grabbed the phone right out of my hands, along with his keys, and staggered to the car, clutching at his chest, said he'd drive himself if I wouldn't."

"Well, hell. That sounds like dad, all right."

"On occasion, he can be the most stubborn man in the world." Her voice broke on the last word, and she raised her handkerchief to dab at her eyes. "I was terrified the entire fifteen minutes it took me to get there. He reclined the caddy's seat and lay there looking like death warmed over. It's the only time I can remember him not criticizing my driving abilities."

Tanner held back the grin that threatened. "He'll be fine."

"Will he?" she said, her gaze burning into him.

He faced her fully and nodded. "He's in the best place

for it."

"So you say, but I'd still feel better if you were there for the surgery."

"How many times must we go over this, Mother? I'm *not* a heart surgeon."

"I know, but some of these doctors here have names I can't pronounce," she hissed, as though she were being watched by the CIA of Cardiac Centers.

"Oh God, I can't believe I'm hearing this. Methodist Debakey is ranked number twelve in the nation last I heard, and you're lucky enough to live within fifteen minutes of the place. Their cardiovascular surgeons are some of the finest available."

"Are you sure? This is my husband we're talking about here," she said, twisting her handkerchief into knots.

"Your husband, and my father, and yes, I'm sure. Did his physician mention any specific kind of procedure to you? PCI or CABG?"

Celine frowned as though trying to recall the conversation with the doctor. "He said something about cabbage, and a thoracic artery, but I'm not sure if that's the same as what you're talking about."

Tanner nodded, pleased at her answer. "CABG, they call it 'cabbage' and it's highly successful. They'll take a vein from another part of his body, attach it to his aorta, and graft it to the heart, right alongside his veins that aren't working properly. I'm assuming they've decided on the chest area if they mentioned the thoracic artery to you. It's common practice and is highly successful in returning blood flow to the damaged parts of the heart."

Celine's eyes widened as he explained, and he got the feeling his reassurances were falling on deaf ears. He couldn't help but think of all the possibilities, all the things that could go wrong. His mother, tearing at the swatch of linen in her hands, opened her husband's door to peek inside before turning her watery gaze on her son.

He patted her arm. "It'll be fine, Mother. You go on back in there."

She nodded once and turned to go back in the room before her panicked gaze found his again. "What are you going to do? You're not leaving are you?"

"Of course not. I'm going to go speak to whoever's on duty and can give me some information. I'm not leaving this hospital until you and Dad do."

He waited for her to settle in next to her husband of forty-five years then headed to the nurse's station. A cute blond with big blue eyes gave him a huge smile as he approached.

"Yes sir, is there something I can do for you?"

"My father is scheduled for a heart by-pass in the morning. I need to know the name of his doctor, and I'd like to get a peek at his charts if it's at all possible. I'm Dr. Tanner Collins, a neurosurgeon at St. Luke's in Lake Coburn, Louisiana. Here's my hospital I.D. and my credentials," he said, pulling them out of his wallet. "I can get my mother over here if you'd like."

She checked the I.D. and smiled up at him. "That won't be necessary, Dr. Collins. Mrs. Collins has been telling us about you. She'd checked with us a few times already this evening, asking if you'd come in yet. I can definitely see the family resemblance. Here's all the information we have on your father at this time."

After studying the findings, he flipped the last page back into place and made a few more notes to his pad before slipping it inside his pocket. He pushed the board across the counter to the nurse.

"There you go, and thanks for your help. Can you tell me what time we should expect the doctor to show up?"

"You're very welcome. We have Mr. Collins scheduled for eight a.m., so I'm sure they'll start prepping him at least an hour earlier. I'll be gone by then, but I hope everything goes well with the surgery."

He nodded, noticing her smile widen as she aimed a blatant gaze at his unadorned ring finger. He smiled back at her, recognizing all the signs of a woman on the prowl. He turned, carefully concealing his own sneak peak at her ring finger…bare and missing a tan line. Tanner walked back to the room, feeling her eyes on him. Years of experience made him confident that *if* he chose to pursue the situation, it wouldn't take much, if any, persuasion. He stopped at the door to his father's room and turned back to verify she was still watching him. He thought of Sarah, her big brown eyes staring up at him, nodded without returning the nurse's wave, and entered the room.

∾

The next day, Tanner pushed open the door of his father's room, carrying two coffees and a pocketful of creamer. He handed a coffee to his mother with the creamer and sat down with the remaining cup.

Celine poured the containers of milky white liquid into her cup and stirred slowly. "I know the doctor said his surgery was a success, but will Justin be in a lot of pain when he wakes up?"

"They'll give him something for the pain, Mother, don't worry."

"He won't tell me if he's in pain, you know. Just tries to suffer through it because he hates to take those painkillers."

"He'll take these meds, believe me," he said, immediately wishing he hadn't said anything.

"Oh God, will the pain be that unbearable?" She wore a horrified expression.

Tanner put his cup down to show her on his own chest how long his father's incision was. "You can't see from the bandages, but he was cut from here to here and they have to use…tools…to keep him opened during surgery. He'll be extremely sore for weeks, but they'll give him good drugs. I promise you, if he takes the drugs, the pain will be manageable. Every week, every day, it will lessen and in a month, he'll be back to his old self, but better. Okay?"

She blinked back her tears, and nodded, pulling out a fresh linen handkerchief. She dabbed at her eyes again, and he wanted to ask how many of those damn handkerchiefs she had on her. Did she have one hidden in each of her pockets? Was her purse also full of them? He took a sip of coffee and rested his head on the back of the couch.

"Tanner?"

"Yes?" he said, not bothering to raise his head.

"Should I bring in a nurse or do you think I'll be able to handle him alone once we get home?"

"You've got excellent insurance and plenty of money for anything out of pocket. I'd say hire someone for the first couple of weeks. Dad's a big man. He's too big for you to handle alone. No use you hurting yourself if you don't have to. I'll make some calls and find you someone, don't worry."

"Thank you."

"You're welcome." He'd relaxed to the point of nearly drifting off when she spoke again, jarring him awake.

"Son?"

"Yes?"

"Make sure she's old."

"Who?"

"The nurse. I want her old, and preferably ugly as sin. Do you think you can find someone like that?"

His gaze fell on her where she sat with her head resting on one hand—gone was the air of superiority and pretentiousness. "Mother?"

He'd been about to make a joke, but when she lifted her head to meet his gaze he tossed aside any possibility of a snide remark. Her face, etched with worry lines and exhaustion, also mirrored something he wasn't accustomed to seeing there. For the first time in his memory, she seemed insecure. Maybe all the years of her husband's carousing had taken its toll. Tanner had always thought she wasn't concerned with his dad's extra-curricular activities, as long as she got to keep her credit cards and the house of her choice. He couldn't help but wonder what else he'd been wrong about over the years.

"Well, like I said, he's a big guy, so you'll need someone young and strong. I can inquire about male caretakers."

She waved off that idea. "I don't want him getting depressed and imagining I'm lusting after a man. That would be as bad as him lusting over some hot young thing."

He did what he could to hold back the threatening chuckle. "I guess we could always go the other route. How about if *she* is young, strong, and only attracted to other women?"

"Oh, a lesbian. I hadn't thought of that. Hmm, normally I don't approve of that sort of thing—"

"You don't have to approve, Mother. Just live and let live."

"Oh, I know that son. I can be just as tolerant as the next person, but yes…Yes, that could definitely work in this situation."

He dropped his head back on the sofa, allowing himself the smile that had threatened since the beginning of the conversation.

～ッ

Tanner cleared the last of his parents' luggage out of his car and hauled it to their bedroom. He re-entered the living room just as his father's new nurse was getting him settled in the brand new electric recliner.

"How's that, Mr. Collins?" she asked, the slightest hint of a Jamaican accent present in her voice.

Justin Collins gave his nurse a drowsy comeback. "Ahh…I can't believe it took me having a heart attack to get a recliner in this house."

Zoe, a gorgeous young black woman with creamy skin the color of mocha latte and big brown eyes, giggled. "Ah, she won't allow it, eh? My mom's the same way. She says they're all ugly and won't have them in the house."

"All my friends have 'em…" Justin drawled, his voice trailing off into unconsciousness.

"And…he's out," Zoe whispered, grabbing the handle to her wheeled suitcase. "Mrs. Collins, where can I put this?"

Celine pointed down the hallway. "The guest room is

down there and to the left, Miss…I'm sorry, I've forgotten your last name. My head is so fuzzy from lack of sleep."

"It's Powell, but I'd prefer if you called me Zoe."

"All right, Zoe. As long as you call me Celine."

Zoe made a face. "How about Ms. Celine? My granny would whoop me good for being disrespectful if I called an elder by a first name."

Tanner held his breath, waiting for his mother to come unglued at being called an 'elder'. To his surprise, she seemed pleased rather than offended by the young woman's admission.

"Your granny certainly taught you right, Zoe. If you're comfortable calling me Ms. Celine, that's fine by me."

Zoe cast a critical glance at her new employer. "Although, you're much too pretty and elegant to think of you as *elderly*, if you don't mind my sayin' so, Ms. Celine."

Celine beamed in obvious pleasure. "I think I can handle a little flattery. You go right on ahead."

Tanner grabbed the handle of Zoe's suitcase and another cumbersome backpack so she could take the rest of her personal items to the guest room.

She gasped in delight as she stepped through the door he opened for her. "What a pretty room. My Granny would say this place is *stoosh*…that means rich back in the islands, mon."

Tanner nodded. "I heard that before in Jamaica. Is that where your Grandmother lives?"

"For most of her life, but she's been an American citizen for twenty years. I've lived in the same house with her since I was a baby."

Tanner grinned at her. "Ah, that's where you picked up a little of the accent."

"Yeah, I spend a lot of time with her, so I find myself slipping into it on occasion. I can try to tone it down if you think it will bother your parents."

He waved away her concern. "Be yourself, Zoe."

Tanner opened two other doors to show her the walk-in closet, as well as her own bathroom. "Looks like you got the deluxe suite. If you think of anything else you may need, let me know. I'll be here the rest of the day and tonight, but I've got to head back to Lake Coburn tomorrow. I need to get back to my job."

"Just the job? No wife, babies...no girlfriend?" she asked, her Jamaican lilt making itself heard again.

"Nope."

"Boyfriend?"

"Nope...don't swing that way."

She gave him a huge grin. "Ah, too bad! And here I had the perfect *chi chi, batty mon* in mind for ya."

He threw his head back in laughter. "Well, thanks, but no thanks."

"That being the case, I do have a beautiful older sister who's as straight as a highway in Kansas, and she's single. Interested?"

Tanner shoved one hand in the pocket of his Dockers and headed for the door. "Not at this time, but thanks."

"Oh, I see."

He looked back from the doorway. "What do you see?"

"You've got girl trouble. And Granny would add, *"You lub sum'ady kyaan done. Rahtid!"*

Tanner stared at her. "I'm sorry, but what the hell did you just say?"

She dissolved into laughter. "What I said, was... 'Your love for somebody can never end'. Basically, there's someone you love a lot."

"There's someone I admire, yes, but I don't love her."

"Ay mon...Si `ow yu stay? Yu can nuh say sup'm." She giggled at the clueless look he sent her. "Loosely translated, you do, but you can't admit it yet." She beamed up at him, her white teeth perfectly aligned in a wide mouth. "You've got the look of a man with a bad case of longing for a woman. Not any woman, mind you, but a particular woman."

He gave her an incredulous look. "We just met. What makes you think something like that?"

She tapped her chest in the vicinity of her heart. "Sometimes the heart sees more than the eyes. I got the gift of that sight from my mother."

Tanner shook his head. "I won't be rude by calling it total nonsense, but let's just say I'm not a believer and leave it at that."

"You don't have to believe in something for it to be true, Mr. Collins.

He left her alone in her room, wondering if Zoe's claims hit too close to the target for comfort.

Chapter 9

Sarah glanced up from her monitor to see Tanner standing in front of her, holding a square cardboard box.

"I didn't know you were back yet, and is that what I think it is?" she said, recognizing the colorful logo from the *House of Buns*.

"I left Houston early this morning to make it in for work. Had this sudden craving for Caramel sticky buns and I know how much you love 'em." He opened the box, releasing the aroma of fresh from the oven cinnamon rolls covered in buttery caramel and pecans.

"Oh…" she breathed, reaching for a delectable roll drenched in sticky goodness. She bit into it, closing her eyes as the decadent flavors melted in her mouth. "Damn, that's good."

Tanner laughed and placed the box on the table near the office coffee pot. "I had all I wanted so I'll just leave the rest here for you and your co-workers."

She swallowed the bite and licked her lips. "Mm, I guess I'll share." She set the bun on a paper towel he'd placed on her desk. "Thanks, Tanner. I've been thinking about you, your dad's surgery and all. How'd that go? No complications?"

"He's in some pain—he must be because he takes his medication religiously, and he normally hates taking pills." His brow furrowed with obvious concern. "I know it's only been a few days, and he'll start to improve every day, but damn, it's hard watching him go through that. It's hard on my mom, too."

"Is she taking care of him by herself?"

"We hired a nurse to stay full time with him, but Mom still does a lot for him. I think this scared both of them into actually admitting they care for each other." He scratched at his chin pensively. "It's been kind of a pleasant situation, not him needing the surgery, of course. It's just that I've seen sides of them they've never shown me before. It's been…eye opening."

"I guess as couples age they aren't as quick to show their affection for one another like they did in their younger years."

Tanner gave a slow shake of his head, still seeming to mull it over. "My parents seemed to get along very well from what I witnessed growing up, but they've never been outwardly affectionate with each other. I never thought my mother would miss not having Dad around, but she was terrified of losing him."

She kept her silence, letting him sort out things in his own mind. He caught her staring at him and cleared his throat uneasily.

"I'm glad you came by," she rushed, when it looked like he was going to leave. "It'll keep me from having to call you later. We're planning a little party at the ranch this Saturday from about 2 p.m. to whenever. Red's DJ will be there, but he'll have to pack up around six-ish to get back to the club. Everyone can either go home or pick it up at the club later that evening. I want Mitchell to meet all the people that have been so wonderful to me since I've been here. Good food, good music, but BYOB. Think you can make it?"

"I think I'd sure as hell like to try…if nothing comes up in Houston with Dad. Thanks for the invite," he said, beaming down at her.

"Thanks for the sticky buns, and uh, feel free to bring a date." It may have been her imagination but she could have sworn his smile faded a bit before he nodded and left her office.

～

"Bring a date?" he grumbled to no one in particular as he stepped inside the elevator. Yeah, that's just what he wanted to do at a party hosted by the woman he couldn't seem to keep his mind off of, no matter how hard he tried.

By the end of the elevator ride, he felt even more dejected, deciding she'd thrown that in as a subtle message. *She's not, and never will be, interested in me.*

Tanner made his rounds, trying like hell to act cheerier than he felt. A few patients looked as confused as a two-headed turtle, making him wonder if he'd laid it on a little too thick. Mr. Fournet, his grumpiest patient, told him he didn't appreciate the sarcasm. Too bad Tiffany wasn't in today. She'd have been able to tell him straight up if he was acting like an ass.

The last call of the day was the woman who'd lost her infant daughter in the drunk driving incident the previous month. He seated himself and rolled the chair to sit in front of her. Once he completed her check-up, he leaned forward slightly, taking her hands in his.

"From a neurological standpoint, you're doing fine, Beth. How's your frame of mind? Are you having any episodes of depression, sleeplessness, or times when you feel overwhelmed?"

"Try all of the above," she snorted, then bit her lower lip as tears flooded her eyes. "I...I miss my baby girl so much, you know? I still wake up in the morning expecting to hear her crying for her bottle and needing her diaper changed." She wiped her eyes brusquely. "It's kind of difficult to perk up when you start the day out like that, but my days are getting better. I have to believe that God has a plan for her little soul."

"Totally understandable reactions to a loss like that. Do you need me to prescribe anything for depression or to sleep?"

"No, it really is getting better, and I don't want to be zoned out in case my little boy needs me."

Tanner stared down at her, picturing Sarah in her place...one of Sarah's girls in the place of the infant this woman had lost. Just for a moment, he felt the ache of her loss pressing at him. He squeezed her hand gently. "I'm so sorry," he said.

She nodded...the sadness in her big brown eyes

tugging at his heart.

"I know you are, Dr. Collins, and I'll be okay with time. I've still got my husband, and my little boy. We'd been thinking about trying for another child. Maybe we'll start thinking about it seriously soon."

"I think that would be a wonderful idea. Maybe give yourself a couple more months to recuperate before going for it?"

She stood, straightening her blouse. "I'll do that, Dr. Collins."

Tanner placed his hand on her shoulder and gave it a light squeeze. "Keep me informed, and if the depression or sleeplessness gets to be too much for you, let me know, all right? You don't need to deal with this alone. We've got excellent psychologists on staff if you need any kind of treatment in that area, even if it's just to talk."

"I'll keep that in mind," she said, nodding as she walked away from him, still limping slightly from a sprained ankle, another less painful reminder of the accident.

He found himself thinking about her several times that week, even as he lay in bed trying to get some much need shut eye. He even caught himself mumbling a quick prayer for her benefit one night. He laughed about it to himself. God was sure to take his sweet time answering any prayer from a guy like him.

∿

Tanner shifted his Lexus into park and got out of the car, reaching inside to grab his small cooler that held a six-pack of beer, and a gift bag containing two bottles of wine for the host and hostess.

Within seconds of Tanner ringing the bell, Daniel LeBlanc, holding a curly-haired toddler, pulled the door open, his deep voice booming a welcome.

"Hey Tanner, how's it going? Come on in! And before I get too busy and forget to ask, how the hell's your dad?"

"He's good, sir. I think this whole heart attack episode

must've scared the crap out of him because both mom and his nurse claim he's being an excellent patient."

"Oh, yeah, it's still too fresh in his mind. He'll get over all that as he starts feeling better."

Tanner joined in with Daniel's booming laughter. "I expect you're right about that. When he's feeling spry he'll be back to his old stubborn self, and refuse to take his medicine."

"Eating fried shrimp 'poboys' behind Celine's back. You know, I've spent a lot of time with those two over the years." He jerked his head for Tanner to follow him inside. "Come on in, buddy. Everybody's out back through that door."

Tanner thanked him and handed him the gift bag. "This is for you and Leah."

"Thank you! I'll just turn this over to the lady of the house when I can find her. Here, hold this for me, would ya?" he said as he handed the baby over to Tanner. "Her parents are out back somewhere and I think she needs her diaper changed."

"Good God, is this Tiff and Red's?" Tanner lifted the child for closer inspection. The baby, wearing a hot pink romper boasting "Daddy's Girl" on it, squealed with delight as he faked throwing her up in the air.

"Yep, that's Brianna. She's a beaut, ain't she?"

"She's changed so much in two months, I don't know if I'd have recognized her." He gazed at the adorable toddler then froze as he heard a vaguely familiar sound, followed by the unmistakable smell of poop-filled diaper. "What's the deal, man? It seems like every time I hold one of these things, they do this."

Daniel's laughter rang out as he opened up the back door leading out to the deck. "Quick, bring her to her parents out there. I don't mind feeding and rocking 'em to sleep. I've even been known to change a pissy diaper or two, but this Paw Paw draws the line at changing the old number two diapers. That's what parents are for."

∼∽

The appearance of Tanner holding Brianna at arm's length drew Sarah's gaze like a prisoner to fresh air. She remembered how he'd held one of her daughters the exact same way, and obviously for the same reason. She approached him just as Tiffany took Brianna off his hands.

"*You* should be getting used to that by now." She grinned up at him.

"I seem to have that effect on babies, don't I? How are you, Sarah?"

"I'm good, thanks. I hope you're hungry. Red and Mitch started cooking before sunrise." She pointed to a corner of the deck. "Put your cooler down in that area."

He grabbed a beer before stashing the cooler aside. "So where is the man of the hour?" he asked, looking around.

"He's over there, talking to Mel. The two of them are comparing battle scars, I think." She watched their animated discussion for a moment, before turning back toward Tanner.

"Yeah, Mitch definitely looks like he's in the middle of something; I'll catch him later. Are the twins out here?"

"They're napping." She pulled on his shirtsleeve. "But, we have another set of twins here today, a pair of adorable little boys. Look, there they are." She pointed out two toddlers, who looked to be a couple years old.

"That's got to be Jackson's boys. My God, I bet that's exactly what he looked like at their age!"

"You know Jackson and Giselle?" she asked.

"Jackson, Red, and I all played baseball together for LSU."

"I don't know much about it," she admitted, wrinkling her nose. "I do love football, though. A good weekend for me is watching any team in the SEC on Saturdays, and all day Sunday watching NFL. I start suffering severe withdrawal symptoms after Superbowl Sunday."

"Any football, or do you have favorite teams?"

"LSU and the Saints of course, but I watch everything."

"I have season tickets for two to all Tiger's home games. Maybe you'd like to come along some time. I know some serious tailgaters who know how to party."

She managed to pick her jaw up from the floor. "Don't tease me, Tanner. Are you serious?"

His gaze grew somber. "I *never* tease about LSU football. So, can I count on you to come to a few, or do I need to start asking around?"

"Oh buddy, did you ever just make a huge mistake! Now I really can't wait for football season." She clapped her hands in excitement. "I haven't been to Death Valley stadium in nearly ten years."

"I usually try to make five or six Saints games during the season if I have time. Say the word and I'll save a ticket for you. I always buy several at a time. It's more fun going to games in a group."

"I've never been to a Saint's game...ever." It took serious effort not to throw her arms around his neck.

He smiled. "After next season, you won't be able to say that anymore."

She hopped back and forth on her feet, unable to contain her excitement. "Can I dress up for the games? I'm prepared to do the black and gold face paint, cover myself with fleur de lis and Who Dats, while wearing my number nine jersey."

Tanner gave her a sidelong glance. "Give it your best shot, but I doubt if you can come up with anything I haven't seen before. Some fans really get their freak on come game day."

She released a throaty chuckle and gave him a slow nod. "Is that right? Well, it looks like I've got between now and football season to come up with something freaky, then."

He leaned in closer. "So, are you planning to shock me, or just embarrass me?"

Sarah's breath caught at his sudden nearness, and her olfactory receptors kicked in. The sexy combination of Tanner's own chemical make-up combined with some tasteful cologne tantalized her taste buds, making her mouth water. "Maybe I'll do both."

"Maybe you'll do neither," he countered.

Her eyes widened. The hand holding her drink froze in mid-air, halfway to her lips. "Is that a dare?"

One eye squinted as he pursed his lips. "I think it's more of a challenge." He straightened slowly, his eyes pinned on her as he sipped from his bottle of beer. "Shock me if you can...Ssaarraah."

He spoke her name slowly, drawing it out like verbalized erotica. She stared, unable to break the trance that locked her to her spot. *The man was pure heat.* If Tanner were an asphalt highway, she would see waves of it emanating from his surface.

A voice from behind jarred her, making her jump.

"Hey Sis! What are you two discussing over here?"

"Football!" Sarah answered, too quickly to sound sincere, even to her own ears.

"The air seemed a little too thick for a football discussion. I heard someone say the twins are awake, Sarah."

"Oh, they'll need changing before I bring them out." She headed towards the door.

&

Tanner waited until she disappeared into the house before extending a hand to Mitch. "Master Sergeant Hebert, I trust you're well."

Mitch accepted it, giving it a firm shake. "I am. I hope you remember the discussion you and I had at the farmers' market the other day."

Tanner finished his beer, and used the opportunity to move the conversation next to his cooler, and away from curious ears. He grabbed a bottle and straightened. "I remember."

"Good. I'd be extremely unhappy if you'd forgotten about it. You and I both know you're not the right guy for her."

"We're friends. Have you heard of that concept? You

know, two people hanging around together and having fun just for the sake of having fun?"

Mitch took a step closer to him. "The kind of fun a guy like you has would only end up breaking her heart." He poked his finger in Tanner's chest and lowered his voice. "Look Collins, you need to go find your piece of ass somewhere else and leave my sister the hell alone."

Tanner's pulse pounded furiously as he closed the gap. "I would *never* hurt her like that."

"You damn well better not, or your ass is mine, I swear to God!" Mitch snarled.

"What's going on here?"

Sarah's unexpected appearance had Mitch backing off and facing his sister. "We're just discussing a few things."

"It didn't sound like a discussion. It sounded like you were issuing orders, except they were about me. I must be mistaken, though, because you're bound to know better than that."

Tanner was thankful she concentrated her piercing glare at her brother rather than himself.

"Look, sis, I know what guys like this are after—"

"I'm sure you do, because you *are* a guy like that, and no! Don't even try to deny it." She lifted her hand to stop his comeback. "I just heard you bragging to Jackson about how girls can't say no to a guy in uniform."

Mitch hung his head, at least having the decency to look ashamed of himself.

"You're right, and I'm sorry," he said. "But I worry about you."

"Did Tanner say we were anything but friends?" She cast a sidelong glance at Tanner.

"No."

"There you have it, but just for future reference, if I was to start up a relationship with a guy, *any* guy—" she poked at her brother's chest. "It would be of no concern of yours. You clear on that, big brother?"

"Yes, Ma'am," Mitchell murmured.

"What was that, Marine?"

He gave her a sharp salute. "Crystal clear, Ma'am."

She nodded and jerked her head in the direction of the far end of the deck. "You're dismissed. I believe Red needs your help with the pit."

Mitch looked over to where Red was practicing a balancing act with a large pan of poultry and ribs. "Oh hell, there goes the grub," he said, rushing over to lend him a hand.

Sarah's throat clearing pulled Tanner's attention from the scene.

"He's over compensating."

"For what?" he asked.

"He feels guilty as hell, for not being around for the whole Troy mess. So he's being hyper-vigilant. I keep telling him it's not necessary. I'll never choose another Troy. After tending to broken bones and black eyes, a little heartache is nothing."

"Is that what you see when you look at me? A little heartache?"

She took a sip of her beer, keeping her gaze locked on him. "I haven't quite decided yet. For now, all I expect is a good friend who's promised to take me to some football games."

"Gah! She's just using me for tickets!" He dropped his head in utter dejection.

"I warned you I take my Tiger football seriously. I know you didn't plan on my pain in the butt brother to run interference, though. Do you regret the offer, yet?"

He gave her a smile. "Not even a little."

∿

Mitch took a long chug from his beer, keeping watch over Sarah and her new 'friend', that asshole Collins. He didn't want to have to tell her about his little underage piece of ass the other night, but if he had to, he would.

"Hey Marine! Want to dance?"

"Absolutely, Officer," he told the buxom red head as he grabbed her by the waist and swung her onto the dance floor. Melanie Finley was one friend of his sister's he highly approved of.

"This is some party, isn't it?" she said, looping her arms casually around his neck as they swayed to the slow country rhythm of Hunter Hayes singing *Wanted*.

"Sure is." He glanced over to where his sister pulled Collins out on the dance floor. Fingers gripping his chin had him looking down into the gorgeous eyes of his dance partner.

"You need to butt out of that, Marine. Your sister can take care of herself," Melanie scolded.

"He's no good for her, Mel. I wasn't here to protect her from Troy, but I can damn sure stop her from getting hurt by that SOB."

"Why do you dislike him so much? He seems like a decent enough guy. Tiffany and Red have both known him for years, and they say he's changed a lot for the better lately."

Mitch caught himself looking in their direction again and shook his head as his sister laid her head on Tanner's chest. "I don't trust him."

"It's not your problem. They're friends for now, and after that, whatever's meant to be, will be, whether you approve or not. I *do* know if you keep up this attitude, you're going to be the one to hurt her. Now shut up and pay attention to *me* or I'll find someone else to dance with. I've been told I'm passably good on my feet, and decent to look at."

He laughed at the innocent smile she gave him and wrapped his arms tighter around her waist. "You are beautiful, both to dance with and to look at, and I apologize. My attention is all yours."

The next song was a rousing crowd pleaser by Toby Keith. Along with everyone else, Mitch raised his voice to *Red Solo Cup*, his arm draped over Melanie's shoulder. After that, Tiffany pulled him out for a Cajun *Two Step Mamou* by Richard LeBouef. He danced with his sister to *Storm Warning* by Hunter Hayes then he switched off with Tanner to get Mel back.

"Hello beautiful," he said, swinging her into his arms for a slow one. "Where've you been?"

She beamed up at him. "Oh, here and there. I had an interesting talk with Tanner."

"Oh yeah? What'd he have to say?"

"Like I'd tell you," she said, with a secretive giggle.

He gave a snort then cocked his head to hear the song better. "I know this song. Is this a remake?"

"Uh huh, I believe someone requested it." She batted her eyelashes innocently. "Who would have thought *Sarah Smile* could sound so good in a country version?"

"*You* requested it?" he asked, stealing a glance at Sarah and Tanner, who were getting entirely too cozy on the dance floor.

"I was on my way to make a request, and Tanner said she liked this song. So, I requested it while I was up there." She jerked her head toward the DJ's set up on a flatbed. "Having your own in-house DJ is definitely a perk of owning a club."

"I gotta admit this is a damned cool party." He gazed down his nose at her. "So what song did *you* request?"

"Patience is a virtue, Marine. Now shut up and dance."

Turned out he didn't have to be patient for long. As soon as the song ended, the D.J. pulled out his wireless mic to make an announcement.

"This is a very special request for the guest of honor of this shin-dig. Here's another home-grown Louisiana boy, Trace Adkins singing 'Semper Fi', his own tribute to the United States Marine Corps."

Even though the two of them started out dancing to the slow ballad, they finished it singing along with the crowd that had gathered around them.

Mitch swallowed the lump in his throat as everyone erupted in hoots and cheering, interspersed with several loud whistles. His gaze found Sarah smiling through her tears. As she approached he wrapped her in a bear hug.

"I love you, big brother. I'm so proud of you," she

said. "But I just want you safe, dammit."

"Likewise, and that also goes for the part about wanting you safe. Thanks for putting this together for me, Sis. This means a lot to me."

"All I did was show up. Red did it all."

Mitch gave her a hug before finding the McAllisters. "Hey, Red, I want to thank you for this, man. This is the best time I've had in years."

"Glad to do it, Mitch. It's Marines like you putting their lives on the line every day that we should all be thankful for. All we ask in return is that you come home safe and sound."

"Absolutely! I don't think Sarah could take it if she lost her big brother."

His gaze found Sarah again, talking to Collins. "I'll try my damnedest."

∽

Mitch leaned against one of two bar areas, hoping to catch sight of the girl who'd served him a drink the last time he'd been in this place. He leaned over the bar to get the bartender's attention. "Hey, is Meagan coming in?"

"Nah, she's not working tonight. I'm subbing for her." The guy looked around the room and shook his head. "It's too bad, too. With the crowd we got here tonight the tips are gonna be good. I know she could use the cash right now."

Mitch sat back, sipping his beer quietly, curious about her co-worker's comment. He swiveled in the stool to observe the crowd, and immediately caught sight of Detective Melanie Finley. She entered the club with a group of people, some of whom he recognized from the party. Gone were her capris and sandals, replaced by curve hugging jeans and cowboy boots. Her sparkly halter-top shimmered with refracted light from the party ball.

The entire group approached, and like steel to a magnet, Mitchell's gaze moved immediately to her significant cleavage. Her copper-colored curls, loosely gathered and in some type of clasp, left the delectable creamy expanse of her neck exposed to every wandering male eye in the building.

He approached, touching her shoulder to get her attention. He suppressed a gasp of pleasure as she spun towards him, the motion causing her bronze- colored earrings to swing enticingly from her delicate lobes.

"Damn, but you clean up nicely, Detective Finley!"

She stood back to look him over and nodded. "I gotta say, Master Sergeant Hebert, so do you."

Already pleasantly buzzed from his third beer of the evening, he could barely pull his gaze away from her eyes, made up to accentuate their already natural beauty. He extended his hand. "Do me the honor?"

She smiled as she took his hand and let him swing her onto the dance floor to a country waltz.

∾∽

Tanner caught sight of the couple on the dance floor and his heart skipped. Not over the sight of Mel, whom, at any other time in his life he'd be drooling over. This time it was in anticipation of seeing the one woman who would have accompanied her.

He scanned the group, nearly groaning aloud as his eyes found their target. *Sarah.* In tight jeans, belying the fact that she'd given birth to twins less than a year ago. Strappy heels, by far sexier than the sandals she'd worn earlier that day, gave her a little more height than usual. The real killer was the barely there, clingy, sleeveless top overlaid with some kind of stretchy black lace. Her hair, in all its glory of golden brown waves, was loose and flowing over her shoulders. He found himself nodding in approval at the entire package.

The thing that kicked his heart into overdrive was her instantaneous reaction to seeing him. The lift of brow, coupled with the slight opening of her mouth was a huge turn on. The sight of her, rubbing the palms of her hands on her jeaned thighs, told him her level of anticipation matched his own. He swallowed, approaching her slowly.

"Hey there." She smiled, and he swore he could feel

the beat of her heart, thumping rhythmically to his own.

"Hey yourself," he said before allowing his gaze to encompass the whole of her. "Damn…"

"What?" she said, tugging self-consciously at the hem of her shirt.

"Just…Damn! You know, as in, 'Damn, you look good!' I…uh…didn't know whether to expect you here tonight. You said you weren't sure."

"I didn't want to ask Leah and Daniel to watch the twins for me after everything they did for the party today. But the girls were down for the night when I left the house and Leah practically shoved me out of there." She smiled, her eyes softening at the mention of her benefactors. "I don't know what I'd have done without those two. The entire clan has taken us in—treated us like family. I owe them so much."

He'd heard her say this often enough, but knew she totally meant it. "They are a very generous family. If I was a father and someone had treated my daughter as badly as I treated Tiffany, I don't know if I'd be as forgiving." Her gaze turned curious, and he decided he didn't have a damn thing to lose by coming clean. "Hell, Red broke my nose for coming on to his younger sister, Annie, *while* I was engaged to Tiffany. Of course, I had no idea he was in love with her at the time, or I may have put up a fight. The point is the entire family forgave me for being such an ass."

Her hand flew up to cover her mouth and he thought he'd finally managed to shock her into seeing him for the asshole he really was. "I'm sorry, I guess I should have told you all this before, huh?" he said, shoving his hands into his pockets. "I'm afraid I'd be hard-pressed to find favorable character references from anyone who really knows me."

She lowered her hand, revealing the smile she'd been attempting to hide. "Did you *really* think I wasn't aware of your less than perfect past?"

"I didn't know, but I figured I'd just as soon be the one to tell…"

"Tanner!"

He stopped and looked down at her upturned face. "What?"

"Will you *ever* stop trying to scare me off?"

"I'm n…"

"Yes! You are!" she huffed, her flush revealing her exasperation. "For some reason, you continue to act as though you don't deserve to have…friends."

"I'm just trying to be honest."

∾

She sighed, struggling to find the right words to break through his impenetrable wall of self-loathing and unworthiness. "You know, Tanner. If you'd only choose to forgive yourself, maybe one of these days you could be happy."

He stared at her, speechless, until the unanswered ringing of his cell phone drove her to nudge him. "Are you gonna answer that?"

Her words finally seemed to jolt him into action. He fished the phone from his pocket and answered it. "Hello?" he said, putting one finger in his ear to block out the background noise of the bar.

His expression grew panicked as she shamelessly eavesdropped on his phone conversation. Obviously, it was his mother on the phone, and from the sound of it, she was hysterical and terrified by something that had happened with his father. By the time he hung up, she knew Tanner's next stop was Houston.

"How is he?" she asked, not bothering with small talk.

"His nurse is afraid he's had a small stroke…a TIA, we call them. It's a Transient Ische…"

"I know what a TIA is, and you need to go," she said, grabbing his hand and pulling him along behind her toward the exit. She pushed through the door and turned to him. "I'll tell everyone what's going on, but you…*You*…Be careful. Don't you dare do anything stupid on your way up there like run a light and get in a wreck or something. Call me when you get there! Do you have my number?"

"I have Red's but not yours. I can call the LeBlanc's."

"My number is 337-555-9104. Don't just stand there. Put it in your phone."

"God, you're a pushy little thing, aren't you?"

"Only when I need to be, now go. And don't forget to call me to let me know what's going on."

~~

"Yes ma'am." Tanner ducked his head and spun around toward his car. He took off at a brisk walk, tucking his phone into his pocket again telling himself not to look back. If he did, he knew he'd find her standing there, watching him leave. She'd see him and that would have made him seem all the more desperate.

Halfway to his car, he heard the quick clip of footsteps coming from behind. She called out his name, and he turned a second before she threw herself into his embrace. He lifted her easily, and she planted her mouth on his, blowing his mind with a kiss that exploded with pent up passion and emotion. He kissed her back, so thankful for the contact, unaware until that moment of how badly he'd wanted it...needed it... and only from Sarah. He eased back, tried to release her, but instead tightened his grasp on her...hugging...holding her. Finally he let go, allowing her to slide down until her feet touched the asphalt parking lot.

"Good Lord," he groaned.

"I know, right?" she gasped. "I have butterflies so bad, I feel like throwing up."

"That can't be good," he said, grinning down at her.

"Aw..." She waved off his comment. "You know what I mean, that nervous, fluttering in my stomach...kind of a queasy feeling?"

He touched his forehead to hers and smiled. "Yeah, I do know the feeling." She kissed him again and he breathed in the deliciousness of her, allowing it to fill his mind, his soul, hoping it would carry him throughout the trip to Houston. *Houston...the hospital...* The wheels started to turn. *Texas...his parents...* they turned faster, spinning out of control. *His upbringing...his womanizing past*...until once more, he was back where he'd started, knowing he was unworthy of her. He gave her one last hug, before pushing her gently away. "I'll call you to let you know how he's doing."

"Don't forget?"

He turned away, willing her not to say anything else, yet wanting her to. "I won't forget, Sarah."

"Collins, is that you, Stud?"

Tanner cringed at the familiar voice, knowing damned well that Sarah's opinion of him was about to take a drastic nose-dive. He turned, hoping to shut the man up before he spoke.

Bill Parker walked towards him with two gorgeous, statuesque blondes, one on each arm. "You're just the son of a bitch I was looking for! It seems we've got a smorgasbord on our hands tonight, buddy. This is Norin and Marin, identical twin babes, here for one week only from the Netherlands." He paused to give Sarah a quick glance, then rushed ahead. "Dude, please tell me you can get a couple of days off!"

Tanner put out his hands and dropped them in frustration. "Parker, what the hell, man?"

"Come on buddy, this is a once in a lifetime opportunity. I mean, look at this! Isn't this the one cliché that's every man's fantasy?"

Tanner spoke through a clenched jaw. "Hey, man, don't you see I'm talking to a lady here?" By the time Tanner turned to apologize to Sarah, she'd already made it back to the club, yanked the door open, and disappeared inside.

Tanner's Lexus climbed the Lake Coburn Bridge at a steady pace, turning the decorative iron pistol detailing on the bridge rail into a blur. His mind reeled at the catastrophe of Parker and his lousy timing. He slapped his steering wheel angrily. He'd be shocked if Sarah ever spoke to him again. How in hell had he gone from the best kiss of his life to this colossal screw-up in less than a minute? Easy…Scandinavian twins and an asshole of an ex-buddy.

He caught his reflection in the rearview mirror, and it suddenly hit him. This was the best thing that could have happened for Sarah's sake. He was fooling himself if he thought he could do anything but break her heart.

By the time Tanner arrived in Houston, he was determined to stay away from her. Even if nobody gave a damn about him, there was definitely some divine intervention going on to protect Sarah.

Could he blame anyone or anything in this world for trying to keep her from being hurt?

Hell no.

Chapter 10

Mitch stirred in the bed, conscious of the subtle, yet absolute change in the room before the click of the door told him that Melanie had left the room. He cracked his lids at the sliver of sunlight peeking through the curtained hotel room. He swallowed, trying to rid himself of the awful taste in his mouth—beer, bourbon, and flaming shots of something called a Bull Ball Buster.

He sat up, forcing his eyes to focus, saw the note left on the pillow. Classic. He opened it:

Hey Marine—it was fun. The bill is settled, check out is at 11:00...I set your watch alarm. Next time you're in, look me up. Keep your head down! ~ Mel

"Son..of..a..bitch…"
Left in a hotel room with a lousy note.
If he didn't know better, he'd think she was a guy. He let his head fall back on the pillow, remembering the night's activities. Soft skin, tiny waist, those delicious D cups, and luscious curved hips. *No trace of masculinity in that particular detective.*

∾

One text.
Dad's fine. No TIA. Adverse reaction to pain medication. Parker was a jerk. Sorry.

One lousy text.
Sarah muttered a low curse under her breath. He'd sent that around noon, the next day. Since then, nothing. She'd hoped for a phone call. She was desperate for the sound of his voice, especially after the kiss. Oh God, that kiss.

She couldn't deny that Parker's arrival with the two Scandinavian goddesses had embarrassed the hell out of her. Right after the incident, she thought, surely, he'd call to apologize for his friend's rudeness and explain the situation. Not that it needed much explanation. The guy was obviously accustomed to including Tanner in that kind of thing. From what she'd heard about that *other* Tanner, there wasn't a doubt in her mind he'd have jumped on it a few months ago. She told herself this Tanner wouldn't have put off going to see his father to spend the night with either of two beautiful blonde bombshells.

Or would be?

He'd half-assed apologized for the guy, yet he hadn't denied it.

She kicked off her covers, got up from her bed to turn on the ceiling fan. She went to the window seat, grabbing the book she'd started earlier and opened it to the bookmarked page. In less than a minute, she slapped the book closed, her ability to concentrate, shot to hell, used it to fan her face instead. Her bedroom's temperature had nothing to do with the heat infusing her body. That was Tanner. Or rather, the lack of him.

She picked up her phone. Read the text for the hundredth time. "Call me, dammit...*Call me!*"

She hit dial and ended it before it rang, just as she had dozens of previous times. "Don't call him, dumbass! He's busy getting his father on new meds, managing doctor's appointments, helping his mother deal with everything."

She pictured him, the look that had come over his face the instant before Parker had interrupted them. She had seen it, by then. The Tanner Collins classic "I'm not worthy," look. "Stubborn man."

He held back to punish himself, because of some misguided notion that he was too jaded for her. She fanned herself with the book again, wondering if he realized he was punishing her, too.

She lifted the phone to eye level and typed in the two words echoing through her mind...hit...*send.*

❦

Tanner jerked the covers away and swung his legs over the side of the bed. He pushed off and went to stand in front of the window.

All his life, he'd been an easy sleeper. No amount of stress or worries had stopped him from getting his z's. Tiffany had attributed it once to his total lack of conscience. He'd denied it then, but now realized how spot on she'd been. What other reason could have allowed him to sleep like a baby while he'd wronged so many people? He'd hurt countless girlfriends and one fiancée by sleeping around, and he'd lost a few male friends by sleeping with their girls. There had been hundreds of them, some with husbands at home. No woman had been safe from his advances, unless they had children. That's where he'd drawn the line. He may have caused problems in a marriage or two, but never ones involving children.

He picked up his phone to check the time again. Two a.m. The phone buzzed and chirped in his hands, surprising him so badly, he nearly dropped it. He stared at the screen, seeing Sarah's name flash. She'd sent him a text.

You ok?

He placed his hand on his chest, trying to stop the pounding of his heart. Son…of…a…*bitch!* How the hell could two little words typed out on a tiny screen, turn his heart into a jack-hammer? What was he, a pimply faced thirteen-year-old, walking around with a perpetual stiff for his first major crush?

He stared at the text, wondering if he should answer. If he did, she'd know he was unable to sleep, and possibly think it was because of her. A two a.m. text message was a good indicator that she wasn't getting much shut eye either. He passed his thumb pad lightly over the keys, then put the phone aside, without sending a reply text.

It's best if you don't lead her on. Nothing can come of it.

"It's best this way," he murmured, reminding himself to stay strong for her. He sure as hell didn't want to be that guy—the one to break Sarah's heart.

He grabbed the phone and put it in the top dresser drawer.

He'd send her a brief reply later, but for now…Out of sight, out of mind.

Once he'd made his way into the kitchen, he popped in a K-cup of decaf Columbian and leaned against the cabinet to wait for his cup to fill. He jumped at the voice behind him.

"Kyant get no shut-eye, Mon?"

"Shit, Zoe! Make some damn noise, would you?"

The nurse emitted a light laugh from the table at the breakfast nook.

"Sorry, Doc, I sometimes sit here in the dark to still my mind from the worries of the day."

He faced her, leaning one hip against the cool, granite counter top. "Do you worry much about things?"

"Keah. A person would have to be heartless not to. I expect that's why you're down here. You aren't nearly as heartless as you think you are."

Tanner watched as the coffee maker filled his mug. "Maybe I just put on a good front." He pulled the full mug from the tray and walked over to Zoe, settling for the chair across from her.

"I don't see any traces of it left in your aura," she said.

He sipped from his steaming mug before setting it down on the end table. "I have an aura?"

"Everyone does. I get the ability to *see* them from my granny. The first time I met you, I could still see traces of it—your former nasty self. As hard as you tried to hang on to 'em, they're all gone now."

"Maybe my 'nasty self' is just buried under a layer of me pretending to be a good guy."

"Nah…no layers. You truly are a good guy." She rose from the table and headed back toward her bedroom. Just before disappearing down the hallway, she turned to face him again. "You shoud be more accepting of that part of yourself."

Tanner sat in the silent darkness of the room, the only sound his quiet sips from the coffee and the soft hum of kitchen appliances. He sat there running lines of conversations over in his mind until his eyelids grew heavy.

He made his way back to his bedroom and settled onto the mattress, picturing Sarah as he'd left her, her last words to him ringing through his mind like the tower bell in St. Louis Cathedral...*Don't forget.*

Not likely, he thought, before finally falling into a blessed state of sleep.

Chapter 11

Sarah dropped the phone on her bed, disappointed to her core there was still no message from Tanner. She brushed back her curls, clasped them in a barrette and headed to the nursery. She could tell from the subtle snuffs and sounds coming from the monitor that at least one of her daughters was awake.

She tiptoed into the room just as two little heads popped above the crib rails, their hair a wild disarray of golden curls.

"Hello sweet girls!" she cooed, lifting Sammi and placing her in the crib with her sister. "Did my babies get a good night of sleep?"

The girls chirped excitedly at the sight of their mother then crawled over to each other.

Once she'd covered their faces with kisses, she changed diapers and wiped away the sleepy crust from little eyes and noses. She placed them on the carpet so they could crawl around. Both squealed with delight at the sight of Leah and Daniel appearing in the doorway.

"Hey, there's my munchkins!" Daniel's voice boomed from the doorway, as he scooped up Sammi.

"Hello gorgeous girls!" Leah cooed, lifting Danni for a kiss.

It always thrilled Sarah to see the older couple make such a huge fuss over her daughters.

Daniel's laughter rang out as the toddler he held patted his face with both chubby hands and butted heads with him. He squeezed her tight and faced Sarah. "My God, I love waking up to these two!"

"What a joy it is, seeing these faces first thing in the morning," Leah added, her eyes creased with laughter.

Sarah fidgeted, uneasy about having to bring up a

particular subject. "I think it's safe to say they feel the same way. One of these days, I'll have to move out of here and give you your privacy back, you know."

"Oh, don't unsettle my stomach before I've had my morning coffee," Leah pleaded.

Daniel stared in horror while clinging to Sammi. "You wouldn't break an old man's heart like that, would you?"

"Come on, you two. We've had this discussion before. One of these days I'll have to learn to be independent."

"Sarah, you had to deal with things the hard way for too damned long," Daniel growled. "Besides, I can't stand the thought of you bringing my munchkins to an old daycare at the crack of dawn so you can get to a job in the city by eight a.m. Why would you want to do that when we love having them here with us?"

"We *adore* having them here!" Leah corrected.

"It's what I feel I should do. I feel guilty. Like I'm taking advantage of you two and taking time you should have with your own grandchildren."

Leah and Daniel stared at each other, obviously shocked by her words, and by the looks on their faces, horribly offended. Leah was the first to find her tongue.

"Sarah, have you ever known us to turn down a babysitting gig for any of our grandchildren?"

"Including these two?" Daniel objected. He jabbed his finger at her. "If your girls grow up calling me anything besides Paw Paw Dan, there'll be hell to pay, I'm warning you now."

"And you know how much I love being their grandmother," Leah added, close to tears.

Sarah stood back, with arms crossed, shaking her head slowly at the two people who doled out nothing but unconditional love to her and her babies. "How will I ever find a way to show you both how thankful I am?"

"A damn good start would be never to bring that subject up again," Daniel said.

"Unless you're moving out to marry some nice young man who's met with our approval and will be a good father to the girls," Leah added.

Daniel turned on his wife. "Why couldn't he just move in here, too?"

"Newlyweds need their privacy, Sweetie. You aren't being realistic."

The two of them headed toward the kitchen, totally dismissing Sarah, who followed, as though they'd deemed her part in the conversation completely null and void.

"We could build them a wing, Leah. How much privacy would they need?"

Leah turned on her husband. "Really? This is a horse training facility in Lake Coburn, Louisiana, Daniel, not Southfork Ranch in Dallas. If you'll remember, *none* of those marriages worked out, and for a good reason. The in-laws were always sticking their noses into everybody's business."

Daniel hung his head. "I guess you're right. Shit!"

Leah gasped, covering Danni's ear and pressing the child to her chest. "Paw Paw! Watch your language around the babies."

"Oops…I'm sorry, sweetheart," he said, pressing a kiss to Sammi's forehead. "Paw Paw has a dirty mouth, but I'm gonna work on that."

∾∾

Tanner woke up, stretched in the bed and picked up his phone. He stared at Sarah's text and sent a reply.

I'm good. Dad's good. Be back in LC tonight. We need to talk…

He only had to wait several seconds before she replied.

Ok.

He spent most of the morning tending to things for his father, setting up future therapy sessions and going over them with Zoe.

By two p.m. he was sitting in the room with both his parents drinking a last cup of coffee before he hit the road. "Is there anything else I can do for the two of you while I'm here?"

"Nothing for me, other than find a decent girl and make me a grandfather," his dad said, wincing as he tried to sit up straighter in his bed.

"Good Lord, yes," Celine added. "We're getting a little tired of making excuses for why you haven't settled down yet. I even had one member of the DAR ask if you were *gay*."

Tanner chuckled at the scene that must have created. "I didn't realize that either of you were interested in grandchildren."

His mother faced him, her eyes wide with curiosity. "Why would you think that?"

He looked around at their surroundings. "Jesus, mother, look at this place! Do you have any idea what babies running around here could do to this house?"

"Do you?" his father asked, eyeing him. "Since when do you notice what babies do?"

"Since I have friends with children. Tiffany, Jackson and Giselle…" *and Sarah.* "I've never imagined you two as the grand-parental types."

"Well, just what sort of people does it take to be grandparents? Parents love their children, and grandchildren are an extension of them," Celine said.

His father grunted as he nodded in agreement. "A continuation of the family bloodline, except they come with the benefits of sending them home at the end of the day. That's what I *hear* anyway."

Tanner scratched at his chin. "What if they weren't of your bloodline?" As he suspected, his parents turned to him wearing horrified expressions.

"What do you mean?"

"Whose bloodline would they be?"

"I mean, what if I married someone who already had a child…or two?"

His mother's face paled. "Is it that woman you brought here a few months back?"

"Angelique? No, we're just friends. As a matter of fact, I'll be a groomsman in her wedding next month. I'm curious, that's all."

"Are you shooting blanks, son?" his father asked. "Is that what this is all about?"

"Justin!" Celine said, her brow furrowing in disapproval.

"It's a valid concern, and could explain this line of questioning, Celine. Are you sterile, son?"

Tanner shrugged. "God, I hope not. If I am, I've wasted a shit-load of money on condoms all these years."

"Now that's enough!" Celine jumped to her feet. "There is no need for either of you to be so crass."

"I'm sorry, Mother," Tanner said, lifting a brow at his father.

"Me too, dear," Justin said to his wife, who promptly left the room. "Are you going to tell me what this is about?" he said, turning to Tanner again.

"It was just a question, Dad."

"Don't bullshit me, Son. Are you thinking of marrying someone with children? If you are, I'd have to advise against it. It's difficult enough dealing with children, especially teenagers, when they are your own flesh and blood. You start bringing in some other man's children of questionable lineage—"

"*Questionable* lineage?" Tanner cut him off.

"You know exactly what I'm saying."

"Are we talking about children or breeding horses or some other livestock?"

"Don't knock bloodlines, boy. Even the American Kennel Club believes in pedigrees."

Tanner clenched his jaw. "Just remember Dad, sometimes when a pedigree is too pure, it weakens the breed—turns a perfectly fine dog into a useless, worthless animal."

"Well, you remember also that traipsing in here

flaunting some floosy and her passel of bastard children would be tremendously disrespectful to me and your mother."

Tanner stood slowly, taking a deep, calming breath. "I think I've got things straight here with all the medical attention you'll need, but don't hesitate to call if anything else comes up."

"Where are you going?" Justin demanded.

"I have a job, responsibilities in Lake Coburn. Patients I need to see." *Sarah...and the twins.*

"You just remember what I told you, Son."

Tanner turned at the door to face his father. He opened his mouth to give him ten kinds of hell as a comeback, then pictured the incision down the center of the man's chest. He snapped his mouth shut, knowing if he said what he wanted to, his old man's heart might just explode. Instead, he took a deep breath and spoke calmly, filtering his words. "I'm not likely to forget it anytime soon." *You pompous, arrogant son of a bitch!* "But you might want to think about doing the same." *Or you may lose your only child.*

Tanner turned, seeing his mother, who stood with her arms crossed tightly across her chest and wearing a curious expression. He followed her into the kitchen.

"I heard more of that discussion than I cared to. What was that about?" she said.

Not wanting to stir up any trouble, he remained silent and grabbed his bag on the way to the door.

"Tanner!" she hissed, following him outside and jerking him by the arm.

He threw his bag into the trunk of his car and shut it before turning on her. "What Mother? What do you want me to say?"

"That you'll come back!"

"I will if he needs me for anything."

"Just to visit? When he's better?"

"Eventually…" he said, after a long silence.

"We want what's best for you."

He laughed. "You know, I brought Angelique here a

few months ago because I wanted you to meet a friend of mine. You and dad treated her like she had leprosy. You're damned lucky that she had enough self-confidence to handle your rudeness with a class that neither you nor dad could seem to muster. I'd never been as ashamed of the two of you as I was that day."

"You're right, son. We did treat her badly, but considering some of your actions in the past..."

"The way I acted in the past was in direct relation to the arrogant snob you raised me to be. I had no conscience about hurting people by my actions or my words. I had a wonderful fiancé and lost her because I felt I was entitled to do whatever the hell I wanted."

"Tiffany never would have fit into this fam..."

"For God's sake, are you trying to blame Tiffany for my unforgiveable behavior?" He stared at the stranger he'd called his mother for over four decades. "If that's the case, then what could you possibly have done to keep your husband from sleeping with any woman with a pulse all these years? And don't try to tell me you didn't care, because it took some doing to find a *lesbian* nurse to take care of the old man—because you clearly cared."

"I...I was afraid he'd cause himself another heart attack if he got all affected by a young desirable woman, that's all."

"Mom...Don't...Don't do that." He locked gazes with her until her façade crumbled before his eyes. "Jesus— come on, sit here," he said, leading her to a bench in the breezeway.

"All these years—I've hated it," she said, sniveling into her ever-present linen hankie. "I put up with it because, well...Who am I, if not Mrs. Justin Collins, the Third?"

"You're Celine Tugwell Collins, and if anybody doesn't like it, tell them they can just..." he paused, not wanting to offend her.

"Kiss my lily white ass?" she finished, repeating the phrase he'd thrown at her after the Angelique incident.

"Exactly!" he said, with a short burst of laughter. "I guess I won't live that down any time soon."

"Oh God, I'll never forget that!" Celine said, covering her mouth as a giggle escaped, then another, until the two of them had doubled-over with laughter. She dabbed at her eyes, finally managing to control herself. "Oh Lord, it feels good to laugh again."

Tanner smiled as she pulled yet another hankie from her pocket. "How many of those things do you carry around with you?"

"Oh stop!" she said, stifling her laughter.

"It's true! You're like a friggin' magician with those damned handkerchiefs. You got some stuffed up your sleeve, or what?" he said, examining the sleeve of her designer blouse. In seconds, she was doubled-over, once more in a helpless heap of uncontrollable laughter.

"Tanner…Stop!" she cried, gasping to catch her breath. "Oh God, I almost peed my pants." She wiped her eyes again and gazed up at him. "I don't think I've ever heard you say the word 'friggin'' before."

"Yeah? Well, we're even then, because I don't think I've ever heard you say 'peed' before."

Celine slapped her hand over her mouth. "I did, didn't I?"

"What? Said it or did it?" he asked, causing her to throw her head back in laughter again.

"I swear, I never knew you were this funny, Son! Where did that sense of humor come from?"

He smiled and leaned over to kiss her on the cheek. "I used to think it originated with me, but I'm beginning to suspect I get it from my mother."

She placed a hand on his cheek and sighed. "I used to laugh all the time, you know, until I married your father. This whole social-status-lifestyle in Houston has a way of sucking the fun right out of everything."

"Maybe it's time for a change," he said, shrugging.

"Oh, Tanner…I could never leave Justin. He's the only man I've ever cared for."

"I didn't mean it that way. There's still time for both of you to change. Talk to him, tell him you won't put up with any more 'extra-curricular' activities from him. Remind him every now and then that he's no better than anyone else. When he gets better, maybe take a trip…a second honeymoon. Learn to have fun with each other. If all of that fails, maybe go to a marriage counselor."

Celine shrugged her thin shoulders. "I guess I could try. I don't know how receptive he'd be to it."

Tanner turned as Zoe's car pulled into the driveway. She got out, carrying a shopping bag and waved to them before going inside. "You want my advice? Talk to Zoe. Really open up to her. I bet she'd help you get the old man to loosen up."

"You're probably right. She seems to have a way of making him do things without him even realizing he doesn't want to do them," she said, giving him a sad little smile. "He probably doesn't remember that she likes girls."

"Nah, he remembers. He probably thinks he can change her mind…him being so superior and all."

"Hm…and irresistible…don't forget irresistible," she said, in a tone as dry as the Mojave desert in July.

Tanner released another low chuckle before sobering. "I know one thing, Mother. If the two of you continue with this little act, you won't see much of me. I won't subject anyone I care about to dad's superior opinion of himself. That means no visits from a daughter-in-law, or any grandchildren." He got in her face. "You got that?"

She nodded. "I got it."

"Good." He stood up, pulling her to her feet so he could give her a hug. "I have to go now. Call me if you need anything," he said, turning toward his car.

"I will, and Tanner?"

He turned to face her again. "Yeah?"

"I love you, Son."

He smiled at her. "I love you too, Mom."

Chapter 12

Tanner headed straight for the LeBlanc ranch, deciding he'd put off speaking to Sarah long enough. What he had to say to her couldn't be said over the phone, and sure as hell not in a text message. As he approached their long drive at the highway, he met up with Mitch, apparently out for a run with Brando, the LeBlanc's Border Collie.

He pulled to a stop and lowered his window to wait for Mitch to reach him. "What's up, Mitch?"

"SSDD, man. You're shit outta luck if you came to see Sarah. I'm helping Leah watch the girls so she could hit the mall after work. Said she had some shopping to do for the twins."

Tanner nodded his disappointment. "Tell her I came by? Ask her to call me when she gets in, and I'll come over then. It's important I speak to her tonight."

"Will do," Mitch said.

Tanner backed out of the drive and headed home, praying Mitch wouldn't decide to be an asshole and not give her the message.

He nearly hit the ceiling when Sarah called him two hours later. "Hey!" he said, anxious to hear her voice.

"Hello," she said, sounding a little cool. "How's your father?"

"The med reaction set him back some, but he'll recover. Other than that, he's a little on the crabby side." *As well as a pompous jerk.*

"Oh, I figured there must have been more trouble since you didn't call."

That stone cold silence after the one statement spoke volumes. He'd hurt her, without meaning to.

"I had some things to straighten out, issues between my folks, and myself." He waited for what seemed like an eternity before she replied.

"And?"

"And, I settled some things, in my own head, I mean."
Another long pause.

"Tanner, are you speaking in some kind of man-code
that I'm supposed to decipher? Just say what you have to
say, I've got to bathe the girls."

"That's the point, Sarah. What I have to say to you—I
don't want to say it over the phone. I want to be with you
when I say it." The next pause was so extended, he
checked to make sure the call hadn't been dropped. "Are
you there?"

"I'm here."

"Can I come over tonight? This can't wait until
tomorrow."

"Okay. I'll bathe the girls so Leah and Daniel can put
them down for the night."

"How about I give you an hour?" he said, hoping
they'd be alone but not daring to mention that.

"I'll be here."

∼∾

Mitchell stared openly as his sister seemed to glide by
him, humming under her breath. "What's up with you?"

"Tanner is coming over, and I want you to make
yourself scarce."

"What for?"

"He wants to talk face to face, although it's none of
your business why he's coming."

He knew she was falling for this creep, and falling
hard. Guilt and bile rose in his throat at the thought of
having to hurt her. Damned if that shit-brick Collins left
him no other choice.

"Listen, Sis, I didn't want to have to tell you this, but
he's playing you."

She glared at him. "Mitch, just because you don't like
him doesn't mean he's not a decent guy. Besides, if he says
what I think he wants to say, he's just going to ask me out
on a date."

"You don't need to be spending any time with that son of a bitch, Sarah. He's a player…I *saw* him."

She faced him. "You saw him *what?*"

"I saw him leave Red's place with a…young lady…and I'm using the term loosely."

"You mean she wasn't that young?"

"No, she was really young—it's the *lady* part I question."

Her brow wrinkled. "How young?"

"Too young to buy a drink."

"Are you telling me that Tanner left a bar with a girl he *knew* was too young to buy a drink?"

"That's what it looked like to me."

"That doesn't sound like something he'd do."

"Aw God, I'm telling you the guy's a slime ball and you won't believe me?" He grabbed her arms, determined to get the message through to her. "Okay, the day I met you and Angel at the diner, do you remember that waitress, the chick with the short, spikey hair?"

She nodded, looking pale. "Her name is Charley."

"That's her. I saw him talking to her at the diner before y'all got there. Then, when I went to Red's that night, Collins showed up, and shortly after, Charley followed him in. Her hair was different from earlier at the diner, but it was the same chick. She had a pink stripe right here," he said, indicating on his own head. "When she ordered a drink, Meagan checked her ID and threw her ass out for being underage. He left too, and I peeked outside just in time to see him helping her into his car. They drove off together. Now, I'm no Einstein, but even I can do *that* math."

She gazed shrewdly at him. "So, if I were to ask Meagan, she could verify your story?"

"You mean to tell me you'd believe Meagan, over your brother, a U.S. Marine?"

"Meagan doesn't have the intense dislike for Tanner you've seemed to develop."

He put his hand up to stop her. "Meagan saw the

entire thing, except she didn't go to the door to see the two of them leave together. Call her, and I'm sure she'll tell you."

∼✎

Sarah saw the hurt in her brother's eyes just before he stormed out of the room. This was too important for her to throw it away because of an overprotective sibling. She knew Meagan very well, and was tempted to call her. No doubt she'd verify Mitchell's story. Besides, Mitch admitted that Meagan hadn't seen the worst of it—Tanner leaving with a much too young for him, Charley.

Ugh, the thought of it made her nauseous, and she vowed not to revisit the diner until that particular waitress had moved on.

She picked up her phone, sent a brief text to Tanner.

The time isn't right for a face to face, Tanner...maybe later.

As soon as she knew the message went through, she turned off her phone. She couldn't bear hearing his voice right now, any more than she could bear hearing her brother say, "I told you so."

No huge surprise she couldn't sleep...the agony of not checking her phone for messages had nearly done her in. At four a.m. she'd completely given up the escape she sought through sleep, and shuffled out of bed to visit the bathroom. She washed her hands, staring at her reflection in the mirror. The shadows under her eyes, proof enough of her predicament. Unable to resist any longer, she picked up her phone. She had six text messages from Tanner. As she held the phone in her hands, it began buzzing. She cringed, letting it ring, unanswered, and then waited longer until the voice mail indicator lit up. Her heart pounded in her chest as she passed a feather light touch over the delete key...backed it off, wanting so badly to hear what he had to say...knowing it would only make her weaker and want him more. Her fists clenched in resolve as she deleted the message, and turned her phone off again.

For the next two hours, she told herself several times over that it was nothing. He didn't mean that much to her, therefore, it didn't matter one bit that he was a dog and slept with anything, as long as it wasn't her.

She went to work, trying to believe the words, trying to believe in herself enough to know she was fine with it. She went through that day, and the next, dodging phone calls, text messages, voice mails, and refusing to check her personal email. He took total advantage of the fact that they worked in the same hospital, by attempting to contact her through her office email. It only took her a few seconds to shut that down.

He must have grown tired of the non-response, because on Thursday, he didn't make a single effort to contact her. At first she'd been relieved, but strangely enough, by noon she was missing the attempts. By early evening, she found herself wondering if something had happened to his father to stop him. By the time she put the babies to bed, she'd decided he didn't give damn about her after all.

Not a problem.

At least not until she couldn't sleep and decided to watch some tube. After a minute of channel surfing she ended up on a country video station. Initially it was a good thing...Chris Cagle's *Got My Country On,* and Trace Adkins' *That's What You Get* lifted her spirit. She was a little somber for Jake Owens' *Alone With You,* but by the time Hunter Hayes finished singing *Wanted,* she was a blubbering basket case. She turned off the set, threw the remote on the chair, and buried her face in her pillow to cry herself to sleep.

∼✺

Tanner finished his rounds later than usual Friday afternoon. Despite a successful week of surgeries and a light patient load, he still found himself staying longer with each patient, conversing with family members, and in general, doing what he'd avoided throughout the previous years of his career…connecting with his patients.

Tiffany caught up with him as he left the lounge with his gym bag under his arm.

"Hey," she said, pulling him to a stop by his arm. "What's up wi…" She took a step back. "Oh my gosh, it's absolute *true!"*

"What?" Tanner checked the area, trying to see what had her so upset.

"They've been telling me, but I wouldn't believe them until I saw it myself. You look like shit."

"Uh…thanks?" he said, turning his back on her and heading toward the back exit.

"Seriously, what the hell is wrong with you? Is your dad in bad shape? Are you driving back and forth to and from Houston every night?"

He stopped, drew out a long sigh, and faced her again. "No I am not. Dad's fine, and so am I."

Her brow creased with worry lines. "Have you looked in a mirror lately?"

"Of course…" He stopped, thought about it, and couldn't remember thinking about anything but Sarah all week long. "No, I guess I haven't." He noted her horrified expression and brushed his hand through his hair, thinking it *was* a little unruly today. "It can't be that bad."

She pulled him back into the doctor's lounge and stood him in front of a full-length mirror on the back of the door. He stared at the reflection of a near stranger…unshaven, hair uncombed, even his scrub shirt was on inside out. "Damn," he said, before giving Tiff a careless shrug. "Well, it hasn't hampered my performance in surgery."

"No, and your patients have been raving about you since you made it back on Tuesday. Your bedside manner has improved a hundred and eighty degrees but you look like you've been rode hard and put up wet. What the hell has gotten into you?" She shook her head slowly. "When's the last time you ate?"

He stared at her reflection in the mirror. "I think I ate lunch." He vaguely remembered rearranging some cafeteria meatloaf from one side of his plate to the other, but didn't have much of an appetite. "A bag of pretzels or something."

She pursed her lips, releasing a frustrated rush of air. "You're coming with me."

"I'm going to the gym, Tiff. I need to work off some frustration."

"You'll never make it if you try working out in this condition, Tanner. You need to eat something."

Rather than get caught arguing with her in the lounge, he followed, figuring anytime away from the condo was better than being there.

Fifteen minutes later, he sat across from her in the diner around the corner, pushing french-fries around on a plate and nibbling at a hamburger. He finally shoved it away and drank the rest of his sweetened iced tea. "Charley!" he said, calling out to the waitress. "I'll have another tea, please."

"Sure thing." She took his glass to refill it and pointed at his nearly full plate. "Was there something wrong with your meal?"

"No, it was fine…my appetite's off, I guess. Just…" He was about to tell her to get rid of it, until he caught Tiffany's glare. "Put it in a to-go box, please."

"When have you ever eaten anything from a to-go box?" Tiffany asked as Charley took his plate away.

"I'll probably feel like eating later. I just don't feel like it right now."

Tiffany sat back in her chair and leveled her gaze on him. "Spill it, Collins. I want to know why your appetite's off and why the great conceited Tanner Collins can't seem to comb his hair or notice when he slipped on his scrub shirt that it was inside out."

"Jesus Christ, since it bothers you that much…" he

muttered. He ripped his shirt off and slipped it back on, over his tee shirt right side out. "Satisfied?"

"You're missing my point. You don't do this…show up unshaved, unshower—"

"I showered." He lifted his arm to sniff at it, just to be sure. Satisfied, he gave her a brisk nod. "I showered."

"Okay, but unshaved, uncombed, and generally unkempt. The Tanner I know would never leave the house looking like that."

He drummed his fingers on the table and dropped his head. "Look, the Tanner you knew wouldn't have done it, but maybe I'm a different Tanner. Hell, you're the one," he said, jabbing a finger at her, "who said I needed to change or I'd end up old and alone." He opened his hands. "I changed! Meet the brand new me, okay? Not that it's done a damned bit of good, because I sure as *shit* can't stop the new me from getting any older, and from the looks of it, I'll *still* end up being all alone!" He hadn't noticed until his rant was over that he'd gotten so loud. He took a deep breath and released it, sitting stone still as he suddenly realized all other noise and motion in the room had ceased. Tanner pulled his gaze from Tiffany's shocked expression to see at least a dozen people, all staring openly at him, some with cell phones in hand. He closed his eyes and turned back to Tiff, wondering how many phones were dialing 911, the local police, or maybe even tapped into the psyche-ward security guards at this very moment.

"Shhh-iiit…" he whispered.

When he got the guts to open his eyes, he saw Tiffany, still seated across from him, wide-eyed, and with her hand over her open mouth. He pushed himself up from the table, straightening to his full height. Facing the curious onlookers, he slowly raised both hands and attempted to look apologetic. Seeing a clear path to his escape route, Tanner made a b-line for the exit. His best option was to get the hell out of there before somebody showed up with a straightjacket.

∽

Tiffany, along with everyone else, watched through the diner's plate glass windows as Tanner rounded the corner and crossed the street, heading for the hospital parking garage.

"Is he okay to drive?"

Tiffany turned, jolted from her shock by the soft voice. Charley stood there holding a to-go box, and a large covered cup of what Tiffany suspected was Tanner's iced tea.

"He'll be okay to drive. He…he's just not himself today."

"No shit!" a man from a table by the door snorted. "Poor bastard ran outta here muttering something about losing his mind, twins, crazy parents, and loving life."

Tiffany gave her credit card to the waitress, then gathered her things, as well as Tanner's to-go items, and headed for the register.

Charley returned with her credit card, smiling as she handed Tiffany a receipt and a pen. "I wouldn't worry about Tanner too much. He's a nice guy and whoever that chick with the twins is, she's a real lucky lady."

Tiffany looked up from signing her ticket to gawk at Charley, sporting a single pink stripe in her short, spiky, black as ink hair. She looked like a kid, barely out of high school. Regardless, she must have sensed Tiffany's obvious confusion and felt prompted to explain.

"He didn't say 'loving life', Doc. He said 'love of my life'. I heard him clearly. What he said was *'I swear I'm losing my friggin' mind, between worrying about my crazy parents, the twins, and the friggin' love of my miserable friggin' life,'* except he dropped the F-bomb instead of how I said it. I don't know him that well, but he doesn't seem the type to cuss that much on a regular basis, especially in a place like this."

Charley looked up to thank a customer who handed her a twenty and didn't want change. She slipped the bill in the register, removing a five to put in the tip jar. "You know, when I was with Tanner last week he mentioned someone with a couple of kids. Everybody loses their mind over love at least once in their lifetime. At least, they do if they're lucky, right?" She pointed to the plate. "Should I throw that?"

Tiffany frowned at the girl who was probably potty training around the time Tanner was half-way through Med School. "No, I'll get it to him," she said, wondering if the jackass would ever change his ways.

∼⌣∽

Tanner had just collapsed on the sofa, wearing nothing but a towel wrapped around his waist when someone knocked at his door. He got up reluctantly, to crack it open.

Tiffany stood there, holding his to-go plate and cup from the diner. "You forgot this, and I really want

to see you eat it."

He opened the door wide enough to grab the box. "Thanks, but I'm not dressed."

"Then get dressed," she said. "I want to talk to you."

"Look, Tiff...I'm tired and I want to watch some ESPN and go to bed."

"You didn't mention eating anything," she said, tapping her foot and looking like she wasn't going anywhere.

He sighed loudly. "Give me a minute to get some clothes on. The last thing I need is your husband coming over to rumble because you couldn't keep your hands off of my buff, bare ass."

"Yeah, right," she snorted as he shut the door on her.

Tanner opened it a minute later and motioned for her to come in. He sat at his table with the box of food and took a long pull from the glass of tea she handed him. "Now, what is it that's got you so freaked out you won't leave me the hell alone?" he said, forcing himself to take a bite of burger.

"Are you in love with Sarah?" she asked.

He swallowed and sipped from his tea. "I like her, sure, and her girls are cute. But I doubt I'm capable of really loving someone. You knew that." He sat back in his chair. "I'm guessing she's figured it out, too."

"Why do say that?"

He took another bite to stall having to answer, then another, taking time to chew. He slipped slowly from his tea and faced her. "Look, I almost had her fooled, but she's obviously come to her senses. So *you* and everyone else don't have worry about warning her away from me." He slapped the cup down on the table. "Just proves my first instincts were right."

Tiffany leaned forward. "What happened?"

He took two more bites of the burger and washed it down with more tea. "Nothing happened, Tiff. And that's exactly the way it needs to be." He got up, threw what was left of the food in the trash, and grabbed his tea. "Look, I was going to talk to her. Tell her I wanted to see her, get to know her better. I thought she was receptive to it, but I was wrong, obviously. I stayed away just long enough for her to change her mind about it." He took another long pull from the tea and threw the cup in the trash bin. "I guess I won't be escaping from my past anytime soon."

Tiffany shook her head at him. "You can't call it your past if you continue to act the same way."

"I'm not."

She walked to the doorway. "Sure you aren't. You know, I came here to try to help. But you're in such a state of denial, you're beyond all help." She walked out, slamming the door behind her.

Tanner stared at the closed door. What the hell had settled in her craw? He grabbed a beer from his fridge and flopped down on his couch with the remote. Some baseball and a few hours of sleep...that's all he needed to put this god-awful day out of its miserable existence.

Chapter 13

Mitch seated himself at the curved end of the bar so he could keep an eye on the door. "Une biere, sil vous plait."

Meagan spun on her heels, her eyes wide with curiosity. "Excuse me?"

"Non, non, non! En Francais! C'est 'Escuse' moi!'"

Her mouth twisted in a cute grin as she pointed in his direction. "How's it goin', Jarhead? And let me just warn you now, other than the English language, I only know one phrase in Spanish."

"Let me guess. 'Uno cerveza, pour favour?'"

"Yep, except sometimes it was dos, or tres cerveza."

He laughed and pointed at a huge canister of mixed nuts and pretzels. "Can I have some of those? What I said was basically the same thing, except in Cajun French."

She used a scoop to place some of the mixture in a small bowl and handed it to him. "Here ya go."

"Thanks." He popped a pretzel in his mouth.

She leaned against the bar. "I kind of wondered if I'd see you back in here. When do you leave?"

"In another week, and I still haven't decided whether to re-up or not." He sipped from his beer.

"I imagine that's a huge decision when you've been at it that long."

"Yes it is. Do I make it a lifetime career, or quit to pursue other interests, other dreams?"

Meagan rested her chin on her hand. "Like what?"

"Architecture, for one. I've taught myself to use cad operating systems over the years, in my free time. I love designing floor plans for homes. I've designed a few for medically discharged Marines and even for a couple of retired commanding officers back on civ div."

"That's quite impressive."

He sat up straighter. "Impressed enough to go on a date with me?"

"Maybe."

"I only have a week of leave remaining, but we could get in a few dates before then."

She tapped her nails rhythmically on the bar surface as she seemed to ponder his suggestion. "I'm going to a movie tomorrow evening since I have the night off. If you'd like to come along with me, I guess I wouldn't mind the company."

He made a face. "Is it a chick flick? Not that I wouldn't go to be near you, I just like to know in advance."

She snorted, shaking her head. "No, it's the scary movie about the two little girls who live in the woods by themselves, except they aren't *really* by themselves."

"Sounds good, so when and where can I pick you up?"

"We could meet at the mall around four-thirty for the five o'clock feature."

"How about I take you to a nice restaurant after the movie?" He held his breath, waiting for her answer.

"I guess that'd be acceptable."

"Is seafood okay?"

"I love seafood. Have you been to PaPa Bill's yet? It's the best around."

"No, but I heard the same thing. Where can I pick you up?"

Her eyes narrowed. "If you haven't done anything to piss me off by the end of the night, I'll give you my address."

"Okay, I'll try not to start any brawls while I'm here."

The corners of her mouth turned up slightly. "It'd take a lot less than that, buddy. Just watch yourself."

∼⌣∽

Mitchell walked Meagan to her door, keeping his arm tightly around her waist in the darkened driveway.

She turned to face him.

"This was fun, Mitch. It's been a while since I've been treated to dinner and a movie."

An interior light illuminated the duplex's stoop through sheer curtains, casting a soft glow on Meagan's features. Mitchell reached out to rub a silken strand of her straight, dark hair between his fingers. "Think we could do this again before I leave?"

"That depends."

"On what?" He leaned in, a hair's breadth from touching his forehead to hers.

"It depends on whether or not you remain in the military. If you do, we'll end this with a friendly kiss on the cheek and a truly sincere 'I wish you the best'."

"And if I retire?"

"Once you're out for good, if you haven't changed your mind, give me a call."

He pulled her closer, amazed at how easy she was to talk with. Mel Finley was fun to be around, but neither of them were that into each other. They'd spent one mutually uncommitted night together and that was fine by him. The situation with *this* girl was entirely different, he could feel it in his bones. It felt right to have her seated beside him in the darkened theater, and across the table from him. Their conversation flowed non-stop, her sense of humor the perfect mixture of good-girl and hotness, combined with a no bullshit, straight-talker.

He nuzzled her neck. "Maybe if you invite me in, it'll help me make up my mind." Her throaty chuckle had his boys down south tightening in anticipation. He sensed, no, hell he *knew* that sex with this woman would be off the charts. "How about we go inside and you can help me decid....*hooomph.*" The knee to his groin surprised more than hurt him, since she didn't fully connect. "What the fu—"

"Shhh…I have neighbors!" she hissed.

"And I *had* a pair of nuts," he gasped. "At least I did until you shoved them up my…" he coughed. "What the hell was that for?"

"You were getting entirely too close, and stop all that high drama. If that crippled you, then you're not the

Marine you say you are."

He slowly straightened to his full height, testing the waters. "Damn, girl! A simple 'No' would have sufficed."

She cocked her head. "Really?"

"Shit, yeah! I don't have to force myself on women, you know."

"Well, I hope you accept my apology then, but the answer is no. If you retire for good, give me a call. Until then, good luck and keep your head down."

"Seriously?"

"I'd never joke about something like that. I have no desire to lose someone else I care about to the U.S. military. There are too many crawdads swimming around in these ponds."

"We call 'em crawfish here, Meg. When in Louisiana."

"Whatever." She placed a hand on either side of his face and stood on her toes to give him a quick kiss on the mouth. "Good night Master Sergeant Hebert. I wish you well, and thanks for the lovely evening."

Meagan leaned against the door, releasing the deep breath she'd been holding. Miraculously, she'd managed to finish a date without her secret coming to light.

Seeing as how Mitchell Hebert seemed to be everything she admired in a man, maybe that wasn't such a good thing. If he continued his career in the military, she'd fantasize about someone she'd never have. On the other hand, if he discharged from the marines—she bent to pick up one of Buck's chew toys off the floor—she'd still fantasize about a man she'd probably never have.

She tip-toed into her bedroom, saw Nik passed out in her bed, one arm draped protectively over the absolute love of Meagan's life, both sound asleep.

Meagan grabbed her Saints nightshirt and some underclothes and snuck into the bathroom. She emerged fifteen minutes later, showered and ready for bed. She tapped Nik on the arm.

Her housemate woke, eased off the bed, and followed Meagan into the hallway. "Hey, how was the date?"

Meagan nodded. "It was good. Did Buck give you any trouble?"

"No, I think he missed you a little but nothing I couldn't handle. I hope you don't mind, the two of us fell asleep watching the big screen in your bed."

"Of course not, and thanks. I owe you extra grande. G'night sweetie."

"Goodnight, Megs. See you in the morning." Nik shuffled off to the second bedroom in the apartment, and Meagan returned to her own.

Meagan cradled Buck gently in her arms before placing him in his own bed. After a few adjustments to his position, he settled down for the rest of the night. Meagan looked longingly at her bed, but knew if she didn't get the rest of her homework finished tonight, she may not get a chance to finish it tomorrow.

Should have said no to the meal and come straight home from the theater.

Considering that both the meal and the company had been totally scrumptious, she couldn't get herself to regret the extra time away from studying. Besides, it was a nice treat. Since going back to school, she couldn't afford to eat out often. She had to focus on the future, knowing things would ease up once she got her tech certification. Soon after, she hoped to have a job that was a few steps closer to her dream of being a pharmacist. Earning her degree in Pharmaceutical Studies was something in her distant future. Until then, she'd study her ass off on her own, maybe take a few classes online when she could.

She curled up on the sofa with her anatomy & physiology textbooks. Three hours later, she dragged herself to her bed, hoping to retain everything she'd read.

Meagan fell asleep and dreamed of anatomy. Not the dissected, nomenclature-type images or charts in her textbook. These taut, muscular abs were smooth and hard, tanned to a perfect bronze, and the trim waist attached to

lean hips. The roped bicep of one arm sported an eagle,
globe, and anchor tattoo framed by the words *Semper
Fidelis*.

∾

Mitch sat back in his chair, sick to death of sad Sarah.
If he'd known it was going to affect her this badly, he sure
as hell would have waited to tell her about Collins' little
side piece on his last day in. But an extra two weeks of
caring for someone would have been even more
devastating. Not that she moped around, crying all the
time. It was there, and the difference between the before
and after Sarah, obvious to her big brother. Even though
her eyes held no trace of resentment, he wondered if he'd
been wrong to butt in.

Leah breezed in from outside, smelling faintly of fresh
air and horses. Her cheeks pinked from exercise and hard
work, no doubt.

"Hey Mitch, we thought we'd have a crawfish boil for
you for lunch on Sunday at Red and Tiffany's place.
How's that sound?"

"It sounds great, but you really don't have to go to all
that trouble."

She poured herself a cup of coffee and added creamer.
"No trouble. I've been dying for some and this is a great
excuse for an all I can eat pig out. I just wanted to let you
know so you could invite whomever you wanted. Don't
worry about the head count, we'll have plenty." She
vacated the room as quickly as she'd entered, carrying her
coffee mug with her.

Instantly he thought of Meagan and pulled out his
phone. He sent a text to the cell number she'd provided,
hoping it was really hers. Within moments, she sent a text
back.

*I appreciate the invite, but I already had plans for the
afternoon. I'll go if you don't mind me bringing along a
date. He won't be eating crawfish.*

Hmph, maybe she hadn't enjoyed his company as much as he'd enjoyed hers, after all. The Marines had taught him to know his enemy, so best to get a first-hand glimpse of the competition.

Sure…the more the merrier. Anyone I know?

Nope.

Need direction, or should I pick you up?

Been to Red's…no need to pick us up. See ya Sunday.

Us…he could hardly wait to see the other half of the happy couple. If the shit he walked in didn't get deeper every damn day.

Chapter 14

By one o'clock Sunday afternoon, Red and Tiffany's back yard was buzzing with chatter from dozens of guests. Most, Mitchell had met previously, but a few hadn't been able to make it to the first party.

By the time Meagan arrived, he'd already had his fill of the seasoned crawfish, along with corn on the cob and boiled potatoes. He'd just come out from washing his hands when he spotted her, hefting around someone's toddler on her hip. She spotted him, and her smile dimmed, as though she'd raised a filtered screen in front of her face.

"Hey, Meagan."

She nodded, keeping her smile to a minimum. "Mitchell. Great turn out. But then, Red and Tiffany always do have good parties."

"He's got all the connections for it. Has his own D.J. and booze." Mitch searched the area, looking for new faces of anyone who could be the competition. "So, where's this mystery date?"

She jutted her left hip forward. "He's right here."

He stared at the kid, and smiled as it dawned on him that *this* was her date. "Oh, hey buddy! How are ya?" He reached out to brush the dark curls back from the kid's forehead. "Are you babysitting for a friend?" He leaned back to compare the tot's eyes to Meagan's, noticing a remarkable resemblance. "Or for a sibling, because his eyes are identical to yours."

She lifted the boy and gave him big kiss on the cheek. "Yeah, I get that a lot. It turns out there's a pretty good reason for it. Meet Buck, my son."

"Your so...?" The breath left him before he got the entire word out.

"Yep." Her chin lifted, a direct challenge. "Scared

yet?"

He took two deep breaths. "I've gotta admit, I'm surprised. You could have said something before, you know."

"And miss out on a movie and a meal at the cost of someone else?" She emitted a low chuckle. "Not on your life."

"Are you saying I wouldn't have spent the time or money on you if I'd known you had a kid?" He didn't know whether to agree with her or be insulted.

"Ah, *there's* the look I've come to recognize." One side of her mouth lifted in a twisted grin. "You're dismissed Marine. Don't feel like you have to spend any time feeling guilty for losing my name, number, or email address."

She walked away, leaving him standing alone and stunned. It took several seconds to realize someone was speaking to him. He turned to see his sister staring up at him.

"Hey, is that Meagan's little boy? He's so cute!"

"Apparently so. I went with her to the movies a few days ago, and she never mentioned him. Nice girl...good-looking kid...but it would have been nice to know beforehand."

Sarah stared after her brother as he walked off to fix himself a drink. Surely, he wouldn't use Meagan's child as an excuse not to see her again. Her stomach rolled at the level of hypocrisy something like that would take in a man with a widowed sister raising two children. She made her way over to where Tiffany and Meagan were speaking and put her hand on Meg's shoulder.

"I haven't seen you in a few weeks, Meagan. I've seen pictures of your handsome boy, but this is the first time I get to meet him. He's adorable!"

Meagan gave a nervous laugh as she hugged her son to her. "Thanks, he's the only man in my life right now. Heck, the way things are going, maybe forever."

Sarah was too used to hiding her own hurt feelings not to recognize it in another woman. "Men can be such jerks, can't they?"

Meagan's gaze met hers as they both sighed.

"Lots of men feel threatened by another man's child, Sarah. I think it must be one of those 'only the strongest survive' instincts left over from the Neanderthals."

"Regardless, you'd think he'd be more sensitive, considering he's got two nieces without a father. The way things are going for me, it looks like it could also stay that way for a while. "

Meagan's cobalt eyes sparkled with interest. "Not the way I hear it. I heard Tanner Collins is turning into the newest member of the walking dead over you not returning his phone calls."

Sarah's breath caught in her throat. "What? Where did you hear that?"

Meagan cocked her head toward the third woman in their group. "We were just discussing a little outburst Tanner had in that café near the hospital."

Sarah raised her hand. "If it involves that Charley, I don't want to hear it. I thought he had more sense than to go after someone barely half his age."

Tiffany nodded in agreement. "I've got to admit, it surprises me. I'm not debating the fact that he's crazy about you, Sarah, he is. I thought sure he was on the brink of growing up, but apparently, he's unable to give up seeing other women."

Meagan's head popped up in interest. "Tanner is seeing other women? Where the hell have I been?"

"According to Mitch you had a run in with her." At Meagan's confused expression, Sarah continued. "He said he saw you kick her out when she showed you a fake ID."

Meagan settled in one of the folding chairs Red brought for the three of them. "You're not talking about the kid with the pink stripe in her hair, are you?"

"Her name is Charley," Tiffany offered.

Meagan nodded thoughtfully, trying to remember.

"Yeah, Charley. I remember that, but Tanner wasn't with her. She tried, but he wasn't interested."

Sarah reached for a plastic football and handed it to Buck. "Not in front of you maybe, but he must have reconsidered. Mitchell saw them both leave in Tanner's car right after you kicked her out."

"Huh." Meagan sat back heavily in her chair. "I don't want to say your brother doesn't know what he's talking about, but that really surprises me. Tanner wasn't interested in her at all. It wasn't an act, Sarah. He was civil, but other than that, he barely tolerated her."

Tiffany took Buck from Meagan and sat down with him. "I guess it's a moot point since he's moving back to Houston, anyway."

The comment hadn't fully registered over the voices in Sarah's head telling her that maybe she'd misjudged Tanner. "Did you say he's moving?"

"He's going back to Houston to be closer to his parents. He turned in his resignation today."

"But I thought this was his home." Sarah could almost hear the desperation in her own voice as Tiffany shook her head.

"He's been in Louisiana since going to LSU, just as I have, but he's got a home in Houston. His parents bought a second home and his is just sitting there waiting for him to go back. I guess his dad's illness was the deciding factor."

Sarah nodded and hoped the smile she passed off seemed genuine to her friends. "That makes all the sense in the world." She checked her watch and stood, feigning the need to check on her babies. She walked into the McAllister's nursery, where her babies were asleep in two portable cribs she'd brought along.

Seated in the nursery's rocker, she stared at her babies and asked herself how she'd feel if she never got to see Tanner again. The pounding in her chest, accompanied by the slight nausea, told her it wouldn't be good. Considering her current situation, there wasn't much else she could do but deal with it.

Chapter 15

Two weeks had gone by since he'd relocated to Houston, and longer than that since he'd heard Sarah's voice. It'd been a goddam eternity since their kiss...and how the fuck was he supposed to live the rest of his life without her?

He missed his friends, and his co-workers. He'd traded the easy cooperativeness of a smaller city hospital for a position at a prestigious Houston medical facility. It definitely had its own set of advantages in technological advances, but of course, also had its drawbacks. God he hated maneuvering his car in and around Houston traffic. He detested spending at least two extra hours on the road every day because of it.

Grant it, the position was only temporary. He'd turned in his post-dated resignation for two weeks from tomorrow. The surgeon he'd filled in for was due back two days after that. The hospital administrator had already approached him with an opportunity for a permanent position. The man was waiting to hear from him before broaching the subject with the board.

In short, Tanner Collins had a mother lode of decisions to make.

The upside had been getting to know his parents again. His father's mental and physical state had much improved under Zoe's care. After decades of Justin Collins' attitude of self-importance, Zoe had discovered a way to knock the pretentiousness right out of him and still keep her job.

The woman had blown into that stuffy old cave of a house like a fresh spring breeze, bringing welcomed change and renewal. Both his parents had responded remarkably well to her down to earth treatment as well as her granny's sensible words of wisdom. The couple laughed and joked with her as if she was an extension of their family.

Celine had taken to setting out tea for the three of them every afternoon. Tanner's first participation in their ritual had resulted in an hour of laughter over Zoe's stories about her granny's antics, complete with Jamaican accents to add entertainment value.

It was a great way to spend an afternoon, the only cloud on Tanner's horizon being that the stories usually involved children. Any thoughts of children reminded him of Sarah and the girls, and that brought on a host of regrets and sadness.

One afternoon, he recovered from the wave of sadness just as he caught his mother watching him, her face revealing a ghost of a smile.

"You miss her, don't you, Son?"

His father sat up, rapt with attention at Celine's query.

Tanner stacked his plate onto his mother's to avoid meeting her gaze. "It's of no consequence. I'm here and she wants no more to do with me."

Celine sipped from her cup of tea and set it on the table. "Did she actually tell you that?"

"She didn't have to. She quit answering my calls."

"You must have done something to get her good and vexed." Zoe dipped a cookie into her hot tea. "A girl wouldn't quit accepting calls for no good reason."

"Look, you two can interrogate me all you want, but I seriously don't know what the hell I did wrong. I think my tarnished reputation finally caught up with me, is all. Besides," he looked at his mother, "I'm sure you wouldn't approve of her. She has two children from her dead husband. He was a real loser from what I hear. I know he liked to beat the hell out of her."

Justin Collins harrumphed in a low growl. "A man who beats on a woman isn't a man, in my opinion." He glanced up at Tanner. "What's she like?"

Tanner lifted a brow at his father's question. "She's a real nice lady, Dad, and she's an excellent mother to the twins—"

"Twins!" His mother bolted forward in her chair. "Boys...girls...how old...are they identical?"

"Uh...I think the girls are around ten months or so, and they are identical."

"Twin baby girls," Celine breathed in a near reverent whisper. "I want a granddaughter so badly."

"Really? Well, you'll have to keep on wanting, because these don't come with papers. As *someone* informed me the other day, even dogs have pedigrees."

Zoe jumped from her chair, her face twisted with a good mixture of shock and rage. "Rahtid! Tell me you two weren't foolish enough to say such a thing."

At least they both had the decency to hang their heads in shame.

"I'm the one who said it, so blame me," Justin admitted.

Celine turned to her son. "I agreed with him, even though I didn't say anything, but I know we were wrong for even thinking such a thing."

Justin raised one hand. "Now, hold on. What if this girl is mentally imbalanced from everything she's gone through?"

Zoe stood over her employer. "I'd say you know your son well enough to know he's a better judge of character than that! Or you should, at least."

"She's been living with Tiffany's dad and step mother for months now," Tanner said.

His mother sat forward. "You see, Justin? Daniel LeBlanc would never take anyone into his home that he couldn't completely trust."

"Not only do they trust her, Mom, but they adore her and the babies."

Celine was quiet for a moment. "Well, that hardly seems fair. Daniel's children are popping grandchildren out like rabbits."

"Mom!"

"I'm not criticizing them, Son. I'm only saying they

have two grandchildren of their own already, and they have two more living with them? I'm...I'm...a little envious, that's all."

Justin burst into laughter. "Celine, if you were any greener, we'd have to change your name to Kermit, and fry your legs for supper!"

Her brow lined with anger. "At least I'm not still making excuses for doubting Tanner's judgment. For once in your life, you could admit you were wrong."

Tanner knew better than to expect his father to do something *that* off the wall. Justin Collins didn't admit he was wrong. Ever.

Justin's gaze landed on Zoe, then his wife, then Tanner. He spoke, his tone gruff and gravelly. "Son, I admit it. I was wrong to say that, and I apologize."

Tanner fell back against his chair, stunned into silence.

"Well. Did you hear me?"

Tanner finally managed to shake himself out of his shocked stupor. "Yeah. Thanks. That means a lot."

Justin gave him a brusque nod. "You're welcome. Now somebody help me out of this chair. All this soul searching and enlightenment bullshit has worn me out. It's time for my nap."

Celine placed her hand on Zoe's shoulder. "You stay here with Tanner, hon. I believe I'll join him."

Zoe raised her brows as the two of them left the room. "All right, but you all be careful back there. Remember, his doctor said no hanky-panky until Mr. Justin is released."

The tinkle of his mother's laughter faded until the door closed, shutting it out completely.

Tanner's gaze fell on Zoe. "Hiring you was the smartest thing I've ever done in my life, Zoe."

"Ach, I didn't do so much."

"That's not how I see it. My God, it's actually pleasant being around those two. They even went to visit Aunt Betsy, my dad's black sheep sister last week. How the hell do you do it?"

"Aw, Doctor Collins, I only shamed them a couple of times when their own consciences were sleeping on the job. Timing is everything though. At first you have to convince them it's their idea to begin with, or they get offended."

Tanner's bellow of laughter echoed throughout the living room. He finally caught his breath long enough to comment. "You're a trip, Zoe. That's for damn sure!"

"Yeah, that's what my mom always said, too." She cocked her head to the side, squinted her eyes. "And now I'm going to be *fass*, that's how my granny says *nosey*, and ask if you plan to swallow your pride and pay that lady a visit?"

"What lady?"

"*Na mek mi vex, mon!* You know very well I'm talking about the mother of those twins."

"She obviously can't handle the man I used to be, and she shouldn't have to. She's much better than that."

"Don't you think you should make sure? What if it's all some big misunderstanding? What if she's just waiting for you to fight for her?

Tanner stood, shoving his hands in the pockets of his slacks to jingle a handful of change and keys. "It's no misunderstanding, Zoe, and this isn't a romance novel. She doesn't want me in her life, and I've got to figure out a way to live without her."

Zoe exited the room, taking all traces of enthusiastic optimism with her. Left alone in the space, completely void of hopelessness, Tanner stared out through the front windows. Instead of manicured lawns and spring blooms, he saw watery images of Sarah and her twins. The words '*...live without her...*' cut through the image like a Broadway marquee. He rubbed his eyes to clear the vision, then placed his hand over his aching heart.

Even if it kills me.

Chapter 16

Six weeks.

Six long weeks since she'd seen Tanner. Since the kiss…God…that kiss. The pain had faded to a dull ache in the pit of her stomach. She'd tried like hell to forget him, had even gone on a date with someone she met through a co-worker. What should have been a pleasant night out with a good-looking, perfectly nice guy, had turned into an entire evening of struggling to focus on their decidedly one-sided conversation.

She attempted to pay attention to her date's monologues, but her thoughts inevitably wandered to Tanner. What he was doing with himself? Was he practicing yet? Was he seeing anyone? *Stupid…of course he was*. Then Richard would ask her a question pertaining to their discussion, and she'd realize she hadn't heard a word he'd said. She ended the date at ten p.m. with a profuse apology, a half-ass explanation, and a promise to give him a call if she ever returned to her senses.

By lunchtime, her growling stomach reminded her that she'd skipped breakfast. Her throbbing head, a symptom of the single cup of coffee she'd managed to down during the busiest morning since her arrival. She pressed her hand to her forehead, digging in her purse for an ibuprofen. A sharp rap at her door, and it swung open to reveal Barb, standing there with her purse slung over one shoulder.

"We're doing lunch at the diner across the street, Sarah. You in?"

"Absolutely…I'm famished!"

She grabbed her purse and joined the throng leaving the office for the walk across the street. Sunshine escaped in spotty patches through a sky heavily overcast from yet another approaching frontal system. It had rained for five days straight, causing rivers and streams in the area to threaten their banks. Ditches overflowing onto streets and roadways caused flash flooding in lower elevation areas. "Are we going to get rained on?"

Someone called from the front of the group. "The rain won't move in until later, around six p.m."

"Wonderful." Sarah stepped around a puddle of water to enter the diner's driveway. "Just around the time I have to pick up the twins from Annie and Drake LeBlanc's place."

Once they'd been seated at the two tables pushed together, Barb turned to Sarah. "Leah and Daniel should be coming back from Montana soon, right?"

Shane, one of the radiology techs, spoke up from Sarah's left. "What the hell are they doing way up there?"

"They're buying some horses. A trainer she knows is retiring and thinning out his own herd. The two of them are on their way back with the four horses she purchased. Leah said it's a long, slow drive pulling that horse trailer, but they should be home by tomorrow afternoon."

"I bet the twins miss them like crazy," Barb said.

"We all do, that house is way too big without them around, and the girls keep crawling around looking for them. When they don't find them, their little chins start trembling. It's just pitiful. I'm going to take video of when the LeBlancs come home, so y'all can see their reactions."

"You have twin baby girls?"

The question, spoken from above, took Sarah by surprise. She turned and froze as the waitress, *Charley,* minus the pink stripe in her hair, beamed down at her, expecting an answer. Sarah finally awoke from her stupor.

"Yes, I do."

Charley's face lit up. "That is so awesome!" She took their drink orders and left, leaving Sarah to wonder how she could have forgotten her vow never to set foot in this place again as long as *she* was still here. Once the food arrived, Sarah's queasy stomach reminded her every time she tried to swallow a bite.

Due to waiting for a to-go box for her barely touched burger, she was the last of the group to pay her tab. She handed the waitress a twenty, wishing she could afford to let her 'keep the change' to avoid any more words. Instead, she stood waiting for the fourteen dollars she had coming to her.

"Twins, huh?" Charley mused. "Do you happen to know a doctor named Tanner Collins? He's a tall, blonde, good-looking guy with gorgeous blue eyes."

Sarah felt the flush creeping up her face, so thankful no one else in the group was around to see it. "Yeah, I know him."

"Sarah and her twins…he told me all about you."

"Really." Somehow she managed to keep her tone civil. She nearly cringed when Charley's face lit up.

"He sure did!"

Sarah's gut twisted. Did this girl have no shame? Pushed beyond the limits of good manners, she couldn't hold back any longer. "Was that before, during, or after you slept with him?"

Obviously, Charley hadn't expected a comeback of that nature. She stood frozen in place, holding a ten, four ones, and some change, open-mouthed and speechless.

Sarah took the ten from her fingertips. "Keep the change, and when you see Dr. Collins again, tell him I said to have a nice life."

She practically ran out of the diner, her breath coming in short gasps to match the wild thumping of her heart. Her temples pounded with pain at the sudden rush of blood to her head. "Dammit!" She covered her mouth, trying to suppress a sob.

"Sarah, I need to talk to you!"

She turned, seeing Charley coming at her. "Please, just leave me alone. She spun around to escape her by crossing the boulevard.

"Sarah…wait!"

The screech of a vehicle's tires on the asphalt roadway

barely registered as something jerked her back from the path of an oncoming truck.

"What the hell, lady! You got some kind of death wish or something?"

Sarah stared at Charley through eyes blinded by tears. "I didn't see it."

"I guess not! You were trying too hard to get away from me. What makes you think I slept with Tanner Collins?"

"Didn't you?"

"I did *not!* Who told you that?"

Sarah raised her hand in protest. "Someone saw you leave from Red's with him."

Charley's brow furrowed in confusion. "I never left Red's with Tan—" Her face cleared as she sucked in a breath. "Oh, they must have seen me the night my shoe broke! He took me to my car."

"Your car? He took you to your car?"

"Honestly! Look, I saw him go into Stubby's, but he left right away. I followed him outside in time to see him move his car in front of Red's place and go inside. I walked over there to talk to him, but that uptight barmaid kicked me out for my fake ID. When I left, I stepped in that damn crack in the sidewalk and broke the heel off my shoe. Like *that* wasn't humiliating enough, I also twisted the crap out of my ankle."

She laughed and shook her head. "By the time Tanner walked out of the bar, I was sitting on my ass massaging my foot. He helped me up and offered to drive me where I needed to go. My car was all the way behind Stubby's and he saved me a painful ten minutes of limping my butt over to the damn thing."

"Okay, but you honestly expect me to believe that nothing happened when he got you to your car?"

"With a broken shoe and a bum ankle? Look, lady. I don't give a shit if you believe me or not. I'm just trying to do the right thing and tell you what happened. We talked, okay? He told me to stay the hell out of Stubby's, go back to college, and contribute something to the world. At some point, he ended up talking about some chick named *Sarah* and her twin babies. I'm no fuc...freak...ing genius, but judging from your reaction, *you're* that Sarah. He said you'd had a difficult time, but rose above it."

As much as Sarah hated to admit it, Charley's story seemed plausible. That left her wondering how to deal with the fact that she, as well as others, had misjudged him.

"Then I asked him if you knew."

Even slightly distracted by the info dump, Sarah noticed that Charley's tone held a distinct 'I've got a secret' edge to it. "Knew what?"

"That he was in love with you, of course."

Sarah whipped around. "What did he say?"

Charley's eyes twinkled with amusement. "He laughed and said he'd only just figured it out himself. I guess that makes you the 'love of his life' he talked about when he freaked in here the other day. I sure as hell hope you didn't ruin it by accusing him of something he didn't do."

Relief rushed over Sarah like warm honey over a bowl of hot oatmeal. This time the sob that escaped was one of happiness. "Oh my God." She planted a hand on her forehead before facing Charley again. "Thank you so much."

"Lady, you're thanking the wrong person. If I'd had my way, I'd have gone home with that guy, and he'd be off the market, permanently."

Chapter 17

Tanner tried to eat his turkey sandwich, but every time he looked up, he found Zoe's gaze locked on him.

"Did you have that dream again?"

He nodded, wishing just once in the last two weeks he'd been able to go a day without having this conversation. He had even tried lying to her, telling her no, he hadn't dreamed that he'd gone to a funeral for Sarah and the twins. She had seen through the lie, just as he knew she would if he ever tried it again. He'd had it again last night, the sixth time in two weeks.

"I can always see it in your eyes, Doc." She pushed her coffee aside and picked up her cell phone. "I want you to speak to my granny."

Tanner growled low in his throat. "I'm not talking to anyone. It's just superstitious bullshit. I don't believe in superstition or magic."

He wasn't about to mention the six phone calls he made to Red and Tiffany to check up on Sarah and her girls. Nightmare or not, he'd never sleep again if he didn't know they were safe.

This time, Zoe ignored his protests, and hit a button on her cell phone. "Granny, he had the dream again."

Tanner groaned at the discovery that he and his dreams had been the subject of conversation between those two on more than one occasion.

Zoe put the phone to her chest. "How many times does this make she wants to know."

He raised his hands to indicate six fingers.

"Six times, Granny."

Tanner listened as Zoe and her Jamaican grandmother talked about his situation.

"A seventh night, and it can't be stopped, she says to

remind you. Also, she asks if you've had the daytime dream yet."

"And I keep telling you, I don't know what the hell she's talking about, Zo. I daydream about all sorts of things, even more lately since you've got me so friggin' paranoid."

She shoved the phone at him, her look daring him to defy her. "She'll try to speak better English for you. Talk to her."

He took it grudgingly and stood up to stare out at the bleak, rainy day. After a single day's break in the wet stuff, it had just started up for another round.

"Yes ma'am, this is Tanner Collins. How are you?"

"Mi betta dan yu, mi teank. Yu had deeay-time drem bout har?"

"No, ma'am, at least I don't think so."

"Hmm…You teank back. Dem allus hapn fore de nyat-time drem. I got de gif ta see drems fum mi granny…she grow mi. Sevn nyat-time drems an sum'ady gweh. You no see har inna di lites."

Tanner shook his head at Zoe. "I'm, sorry, Zo, but I didn't understand much of that."

She reached over and grabbed the phone from him. "Granny, sey agin." She listened carefully and translated. "She wants you to think back. She says the daytime dream always happens before the nighttime dream. It's like a hint at how the dream will come to pass. She got the gift to interpret dreams from her own grandmother who raised her from a child. She said that after the seventh dream of the same thing, it'll be too late to stop it. *'Sum'ady gweh.'* That means 'somebody will go away' or they'll die and you won't see her tomorrow or any other day." She put the phone to her ear and listened again. "She says the daydream may be a very brief vision that may only last a second or two."

Tanner stood looking out the front windows at his parents' rain soaked lawn, and suddenly got a feeling of Deja vu. He calmed his mind, willing the memory to come to him, and it finally did. He had been staring out of these same windows, and had seen…what was it? Wavy images of Sarah and her twins and the words '...*live without her...* '

"Wavy images of Sarah…wavy…" Sounds of the five o'clock local news cut into his musings.

"Flash flood warnings are in effect for areas of southeast Texas and southwest Louisiana. Good evening. A Liberty county woman was rescued from certain death when strong currents swept her car into a local stream swollen and overflowing with floodwaters. Too much rain has caused dangerous and deadly situations in both Texas and our neighbor to the east, Louisiana."

"Wavy images…watery…Jesus Christ!" A cold dread passed over him as he put it together. "Live without her…It's water, Zo. It's the flood waters. They're in danger of drowning!"

∾

Sarah heard her cell ringing insistently in her purse. No way would she take her hands off the steering wheel. Her girls, both buckled safely in car seats in the back of Leah's Explorer, chewed quietly on teething rings and chatted away to each other. Leah had called last night, insisting she take her truck rather than Sarah's lower profile car. *You're liable to run into some water on those back roads, Sarah. You'll be safer in my Explorer.*

"No kidding," she groaned, stopping the truck to peer out into the fast approaching darkness.

As far as she could see ahead of her, water had covered the road completely. She couldn't distinguish the edge of roadway from the ditches on either side. She knew she was approximately halfway between Tiffany and Red's ranch and Leah and Daniel's place.

"God, why didn't I pull into their driveway?" She thought about going back, but stared into the rearview camera at a strong current rushing behind the truck. "Oh shit," she breathed. "Where the hell did *that* come from?"

She dug her phone out of her purse, saw that she had seven missed calls, a decent signal, but a weak battery. Too panicked to do anything else, she hit the call back button. Tanner answered on the second ring, sounding every bit as panicked as she felt.

"Sarah, where are you?"

"I'm about halfway between Red's drive and Daniel's, Tanner. The water is coming over the road, and I'm too afraid to try and turn around."

"Don't move! I'm on my way there!"

"What do you mean? Where are you?" She heard the panic in her own voice rising as quickly as the water surrounding her and her babies. "Oh God, why didn't I just stay at Annie and Drake's place?"

"I'm nearly at Red's driveway, but I don't think my car will make it."

"Your Lexus is too low to the ground, Tanner. I'm in Leah's Explorer, and the water is about to cover the lights!" she shrieked.

"Sarah…listen to me. I'm going to let you go so I can call Red, but I will call you back."

"No! Please don't hang up! I'm afraid." She nearly screamed once she realized he'd hung up already. The two minutes it took for him to call back dragged on with nothing to do but watch the water rise. She did remember to plug her phone into the charger.

She hit the button to accept his call immediately. "Tanner?"

"We're coming. Stay where you are though, don't try to get out of the vehicle."

She stared out at the terrifying sight of water rushing around the truck. "How could I, Tanner? I have two babies with me."

"You'll be fine. I see Red coming to meet me in his truck."

She turned around in her seat to watch her babies, one starting to nod off while the other chatted away. "Oh God! Trying to get out of here with the two of them would be impossible."

"Not with me there to help you. Hang on, I need to get

to Red's truck, but I won't hang up, I promise."

She stared at her babies, knowing that any minute the water could carry all of them off. She clung to the phone as though it were her lifeline, hearing lots of static, swearing, and yelling, as well as the sound of rushing water.

"Sarah?"

As soon as he spoke, she felt the truck shift slightly. "Oh God!" She sobbed, her chest aching with terror as the dark, dreary evening fully surrounded her.

"Sarah, we're coming!"

She turned the beams on high, realizing they were already under water. "Tanner the lights are under water…and…and the truck is starting to shift. Oh God, I have to get my babies out of here!"

"Sara, listen to me. We're almost there. Get in the back seat with them. Do that now."

Tanner's voice, deep, controlled, and soothing, had a calming effect on her. She crawled into the back seat with the girls, bringing her purse with her. "Okay, I'm in the back seat."

"Look behind you Sarah! We're right here!"

"I see you! Oh God, I see the headlights…"

"Here's what I need you to do, sweetie. Turn on the overhead light if it works."

She flipped on the light, releasing a small prayer of thanks as light bathed the interior of the cab.

"Okay, good. Is the water up to the windows yet?"

"It's just below it, Tanner, but it's rising." She heard Red say something in the background about the window on the cargo lift.

"We're going to pull up right behind you, Sarah. I want you to take the girls out of their car seats. I want all of you in the cargo area of the truck. You'll hand me the girls one at a time, through the open window, and I'll bring them to Red. I'll carry you to the truck last, and Sarah, we need to do this as quickly as possible. We don't want Red's truck to stall. He's got a boat in the back, but he'd just as soon not lose the truck if he doesn't have to."

"Okay." She put one baby in the cargo area, then crawled in back with the second. Danni, who'd been drifting off needed some comforting while Sammi crawled around the cargo space like it was her personal playpen on wheels.

Sarah breathed a sigh of relief as Red's huge work truck pulled up slowly behind them and stopped, with a good majority of the vehicle above water. She unlatched the hatchback window, well above the water line, and pushed it open manually. Seconds after she heard the slam of a truck door, Tanner appeared at the window.

"Here!" She handed Danni to him and got Sammi ready. As soon as Tanner left with Sammi, Sarah looped the diaper bag and her purse around her neck. Deciding to make it easier on Tanner, she climbed out, balancing herself on the rear bumper.

～～

Tanner handed Sammi to Red and turned to see Sarah standing awkwardly on the rear bumper. "Stay there!" He swore under his breath and struggled to make it to her in the strengthening current of rising water. When he was only two steps from the Explorer, Sarah's foot slipped and she plunged into the murky water. He dove for her and grabbed hold of her thrashing arm.

"Gotcha!" he said, as she came up coughing and sputtering. He picked her up, slightly more awkward now that she was thoroughly saturated and shivering like a wet dog. "Didn't I tell you to stay put?"

"I w—w—anted to m—ma—ake it easier for y—you."

It took all his concentration and effort to get them both safely back to the truck. The water was nearly waist high on him and filled with floating debris.

"Get the door," he said. She pulled it open and he deposited her in the back of Red's truck before he climbed in beside her. As soon as they were safely inside, he took both babies from the driver.

"Get us outta here, buddy. I don't know where the hell

all that water's coming from, but it's rising and that current is a bitch."

"G—give me one." Sarah's teeth chattered as she reached for Sammi. "What ab—bout Leah's t—truck?"

Red cleared his throat. "Um…you mean that one?" The three of them sat there long enough to watch an uprooted tree slam into the Explorer. It pushed it off the roadway into the much deeper ditch.

Without another word, Red threw his truck in reverse and backed up slowly until he found a spot elevated enough to turn around. It took another five minutes to make it back to their ranch. Even with the truck's rear seat heater blasting warm air onto them, Sarah's teeth chattered uncontrollably. Tanner figured it had as much to do with her nerves as from being wet and cold.

Tiffany McAllister, near hysterical from worrying about the woman she treated as the sister she never had, pulled her into her arms for a hug.

"Thank God you're all safe! You should have come straight here instead of trying to make it to Dad's, Sarah. That stretch of road is so close to the bayou."

Sarah spoke through chattering teeth. "I kn—know b—better n—now."

"You…hot shower…now!" She pointed to the hallway leading to the master suite. "I'll find you some dry clothes."

"B—but the t—tw—ins n—eed their s—su—upper."

Tanner placed his hands on her shoulders and nudged her toward the hallway. "The girls will be fine, Sarah. Go tend to yourself."

Tiffany herded her into the bedroom, but before the door shut, Sarah turned back to Tanner and smiled. She mouthed the words 'thank you' and disappeared.

～〜

He stepped out of the guest bath clean, dry and dressed in clothes borrowed from Red. He was in the process of adjusting himself when a soft click from his left drew his attention. He turned in time to see Sarah, standing at the nursery door, wearing a soft yellow sundress. From the look on her face, he figured she'd seen his last adjustment. "Sorry, I'll wear a pair of McAllister's jeans, but I won't subject my boys to another man's boxer briefs. Not much for going commando."

She nodded, her eyes sparkling with laughter. "I understand."

"You okay?" He took two steps closer then rested one shoulder against the wall.

She pushed her freshly blow-dried hair back from her face and nodded. "Much. Still kind of in shock, I guess. Also still trying to figure out how you managed to find us when you did."

"That's a long story that can wait for another day."

"That may be, but what I have to say to you can't wait." She pointed to the empty guestroom. "Can we go in there and talk?"

He followed her inside, somewhat surprised when she closed and locked the door behind them.

She faced him, fidgeting with her hands before taking a deep breath. "I know you may find this difficult to believe, but I was going to call you as soon as I got home tonight."

He crossed his arms and leaned against the wall. "After all this time? Why tonight?"

"I wanted to apologize for misjudging you. Someone saw you leaving Red's with Charley one night. You know, Charley from the diner by the hospital?"

Tanner straightened, ready to defend himself. "I only brought her to her car. Her shoe heel snapped off, and she twisted her ankle."

She raised her hand to stop him. "I know. I spoke to her today, and she told me everything. It seems she knew about me."

He dropped his arms. "I may have mentioned you. So, you're telling me you've been putting me through hell by not answering my calls, or returning my calls or emails because you believed some trash talk about me."

"Pretty much sums it up."

He took a step closer. "Sounds like you've got some heavy apologizing to do. So, when do you plan to start all this making up for lost time?"

She stepped into him. "I thought I'd start right now if it's all right with you."

He scratched at his chin. "I don't know. I'd hate to give you the impression that I'm easy."

She frowned. "Well, I hadn't planned to apologize by throwing myself at you. Then you'd think *I* was easy."

"Uh uh, I promise I would never think that!"

Her laughter filled the room as he pulled her close for a kiss, the first since that night in front of Red's club. This kiss was soft and prolonged, a huge change from their first; that one was hurried, desperate, filled with longing because they had both known he had to leave. This kiss left him aching, hard as a rock, and wanting more. He pulled away, not wanting her to think he *only* wanted her body. She followed, her actions as well as her words, quelling his fear.

"Please don't pull away from me." Her hands slipped around his waist to press herself against him.

He sucked in his breath, struggling for control. "I was trying to be a gentleman."

Her lips pursed in a pretty little pout. "But I want *you*."

Tanner chuckled as he relaxed, letting her feel the strength of his need for her. "Hell, Sarah, I was afraid to scare you off."

Dark lashes fluttered against her flushed cheeks. "I don't scare easily."

"That's nice to know, but I bet I've got something that'll scare you."

She sat on the foot of the bed, pulled him down beside her. "Don't disappoint me, Tanner."

He brushed her hair back, cupping her face in his hands. "I love you, Sarah." He waited for some kind of shock on her part, or regret on his own, and got neither. "I want you in my life. I want to be a father to your girls, a husband to you. I want us to be a family. I love you."

She kissed him again, pressing herself against him, telling him, without words, how much she wanted him too. He shivered as a wave of need hit him hard. "I'm warning you now. I'll be like a horny teenager around you."

Her laughter, low in her throat, had a seductive lilt to it. "I wouldn't have it any other way. Besides, I know just what to do with that."

His breath caught in his throat as she rubbed his erection through the jeans. "You do?"

"Uh huh. I plan on loving you so much you'll be willing to wait for it."

"I'd wait for you if that's what you want. I would, Sarah." He released a shaky breath, trembling with a fifty/fifty jolt of desire and happiness.

Sarah pushed him back on the bed and stretched out beside him, her head supported by one hand and elbow. "I know you *would*," she whispered, in a voice husky with desire.

Her free hand slipped under the front of his tee shirt to skim the panes of his abs. She leaned forward to kiss him, the soft scent of floral shampoo teasing him as her hair brushed his face. Her hand slipped down to the waistband of his borrowed jeans. In seconds, she had him unsnapped and unzipped, and totally exposed.

"But you won't have to…"

Chapter 18

Sarah sat back against the arm of the couch, her knees bent and resting on Tanner's lap as he leaned comfortably against her. Her daughters' giggles carried from the other side of the room where Celine and Zoe sat on the floor playing with them.

Sammi pulled herself up by Zoe's shoulder, then took three steps toward Celine before falling on her butt.

Celine's screech of excitement overrode Sammi's frustrated cry. "She walked! Did you see that? She walked!"

"What?!" Tanner bolted upright and Sarah followed suit. "She did not!"

"Yes, she did." Zoe put her head back and laughed. "*Dat beeny baybee* took three steps trying to get to her granny."

Celine scooped up the child. "Granny is so proud of you, my little pumpkin!"

Danni, seeing her sister getting extra attention from their surrogate grandmother, scrunched her face and crawled over to them. She pulled up on Celine, her mouth open to plaster sloppy, wet kisses on her face.

Celine's laughter rang out in the large room. "Oh, thank you, my love. Those are such good sugars and you know granny loves her sugars."

Tanner shook his head. "Unbelievable! I've been practically standing on my head to get one of them to take a step for two weeks now and she walks to you?"

Celine hugged both girls to her, and beamed at her son. Well, Son, I guess you don't have the touch yet."

Sarah took her growling fiancé's arm and walked with him over to where the twins were drooling all over his mom. "Now you know how I felt when *you* found their first teeth just after we moved in with Leah and Daniel."

"Speaking of those two, how are they? Have they forgiven you yet for moving into your own place?"

"They're fine, and yes, but only because I consented to let them babysit the twins when I'm at work. Leah said Daniel moped around the house for an entire week."

"Well, it's no wonder," Celine gushed. "Now that I see how attached I am to these precious girls I know it must have broken their hearts to have you move out."

She turned to Tanner. "And I didn't know you found their first teeth."

"Yes, I did." He crouched down about three feet from them and put his hands out. "And I bought them each a new outfit for good luck, didn't I, baby girls? Now, come on. Walk to me. Walk to Tanner."

Both girls squealed at the sight of him and stepped in place, but wouldn't let go of Celine.

Eyes gleaming with determination, Tanner got down on his knees. "Come on, Sammi, walk to me…Walk to daddy!"

The toddler waved her hands and took a step then wobbled as everyone gasped. She balanced herself before reaching out to him, then took three more steps to fall into his arms.

He held her up in the air. "*That's* daddy's big girl! Now it's your sister's turn." He reached one arm out to Danni. "Come on Danni. Walk to daddy!"

After another minute of his and Sarah's coaxing, Danni took five wobbly steps toward them. She stopped in front of the two of them, looked at Sarah, then Tanner, before lunging toward his outstretched arm. He burst into laughter as he got to his feet, his arms full up with smiling, drooling babies. "How do you like that, Mommy?"

Sarah stared at him, her sight blurry from tears, wondering if he'd even noticed that he'd suddenly gone from Tanner to 'Daddy'. "I love it. And I love you." She moved in close for a group hug.

Tanner surrendered Sammi to her before pulling Sarah close for a kiss. "I love you too, Babe."

Justin Collins' booming voice accompanied his entrance into the room. "Where's my girls? I've been stuck in that stupid old doctor's office all afternoon. I wanted to reschedule to another day, but no! Granny wouldn't let me." He grabbed both babies and walked around, bouncing them in his arms, speaking in secretive tones. "I think she and Zoe didn't want me here so they could have you all to themselves. It's a conspiracy, I tell you."

Celine put her hands on her hips. "Of course, Justin. You found us out. We conspired to have you go in for your monthly check-up. Now, what did the stupid old doctor have to say?"

"The same thing he always says. I'm doing great for an old fart and he wishes he was half as good-looking as me."

Celine rolled her eyes and groaned. "Come on, sweetie, what'd he really say?"

"Oh all right. He gave me a clean bill of health and said I could resume all normal activities." He leaned over and gave his wife a quick kiss on the lips. "Did you hear that Dear? *All* normal activities."

Celine pulled her husband close for another kiss and purred. "Now that does sound promising. I hope we haven't forgotten."

"It'll come back to us. Just like riding a bike." A naughty lift of his brow accompanied his next comment. "Or riding something el—"

"Whoa!" Tanner cleared his throat noisily. "Dear *God*, please don't make me listen to the rest of this conversation! Babe, are you up for that trip to the mall now? You know, the girls are outgrowing all of their clothes."

Celine giggled like a school-girl and pushed away from her husband. "No, no! We'll have plenty of time for that after the four of you go back to Lake Coburn. But how about if Justin, Zoe and I take the girls shopping and give you and Sarah the afternoon to yourselves?"

Tanner turned to Sarah. "That sounds like an offer I don't want to pass up. What do you think, mom?"

The thought of being alone with Tanner had her salivating over the possibilities. "I think I'd be very grateful for a little us time. Are you sure y'all can handle this, Celine? You practically have to pack a suitcase to go anywhere with them."

"Oh, I think we can handle it for, say, two or three hours?" Celine reached over to pat Sarah's arm, giving her a conspiratorial smile.

Sarah's heart skipped at the thought of that much time with Tanner. "*Three* hours would be lovely, Celine, and thank you, *so* much."

"Oh, honey. It's the least we can do. You and these darling girls have brought such a ray of sunshine into our lives. We are so honored for the chance to be a part of yours."

Sarah's eyes welled up with tears, and she gave her future mother-in-law a huge hug.

This time it was Justin's throat-clearing *harrumph* that broke up the touching scene. "Okay, we'd better get moving before somebody else buys up all the good stuff. Pops only wants the prettiest clothes for his two girls."

Sarah smiled through more tears as 'Pops' attempted to wipe his own eyes without being noticed.

Ten minutes later, she and Tanner stood at the door, waving to the departing Navigator.

"God, your parents are a trip."

"They haven't always been this way, you know." Tanner closed the door and locked it, before turning to her, wearing a lecherous grin.

Sarah settled into his kiss with a long, languid sigh. God, she loved kissing this man. Tanner had a way of making her want him with a single look, the slightest touch, but his kisses…one kiss from him had her tingling, practically trembling with need, in mere seconds. She pulled slowly away, letting her hand travel down the length of him to settle on his thick, hard bulge.

He sucked in his breath and reached out for her. "Mm

hmm, you're in some kind of trouble now, lady."

She avoided his grasp, ripped her shirt over her head and threw it at him. "Prove it!"

He lunged at her and she screeched as she slipped past him, heading to the guest suite. He followed, grabbing her from behind and dropping to the bed with her. The frantic struggle to rid themselves of anything creating a barrier between skin to skin, resulted in a pile of discarded threads and a tangle of bare limbs.

"Wait!" She pulled back, breathless, perched above him. "Can I just say how happy it made me to hear you call yourself 'daddy'? Did you even notice it when you said it?"

He smiled, lifted her easily, placing her astride him. "Honestly? It felt so natural I didn't notice it at first. Once I did, I liked the sound of it. I've been meaning to ask if you'd mind."

"Of course not. I'd wondered if you even wanted them to call you 'Daddy'. I mean, calling you Tanner would have been perfectly acceptable."

He frowned. "Not to me. When I marry you, those girls will be every bit mine as they are yours. I want to adopt them, and I sure as hell will not let any daughter of mine call me anything other than Daddy." He pulled her close for a kiss. "You'll just have to take my word for how much of a stretch this is for me, but I love it, and I love you so damn much, it hurts."

She leaned forward, letting her hair drape across his sculpted abs. "But, I don't want you to hurt, Tan."

"Then you'd better do something quick because I've got a stiff so hard it's killing me." He sucked in his breath when she wrapped her hand around it.

"You mean this? This old thing right here?" She couldn't keep the laughter from her voice or the smile from her face.

He spoke through gritted teeth. "Fair warning...any minute that *old thing* could go off."

She raised herself, slowly and settled onto him,

adjusting for the closest, tightest possible fit, sighed when she found it. "Ooooh…beautiful," she breathed.

~~

Tanner stared in complete awe at the woman who'd totally transformed him, his life, his entire world. Her hands splayed on his chest, her head thrown back, her bare neck arched gracefully. He reached up, placing his hands on breasts that some men would consider far from perfect. Those breasts had given nourishment to not one, but two beautiful baby girls. To him they were perfection. "Yes, you are."

She lowered her face to stare down at him with eyes filled with emotion. "Marry me, Tanner."

He lifted her left hand, holding the engagement ring he'd given her two months earlier. "I've done my part. I'm waiting for you to say when."

"When."

He shook his head. They'd played this game before. "Not good enough…I want a date."

"This weekend. Tomorrow. Tonight. Right now…I don't care, as long as it's soo…oo...oon." She began moving against him, setting up a slow rhythm.

He kept his eyes on her, rubbing her nipples in slow, circular motions with the pads of his thumbs, arching his hips to meet hers. Determined to set this deal in stone, he lowered one hand to where their bodies met, found the spot he wanted and softly manipulated until he had her writhing on top of him. "Tomorrow?"

She moaned, obviously distracted. "Hmmmm?"

This was just the way he wanted her…Too turned on to think. "Tomorrow. Marry me tomorrow, Sarah. We could always have a big wedding later. Jackson and Red both did that."

"Mm, I just, I just want you."

Her face flushed suddenly, a sure sign she was close. He knew what he wanted her to say, and he knew exactly *when* he wanted her to say it. He increased the intensity of his thrusts, all his concentration on her now, wanting her to reach her limit, without a care for his own needs. What he needed was a word, one simple word. He gave her another minute. "That's it. That's it, Sarah. You're so close now." Her moans turned to soft whimpers, the sound he'd been waiting for. "So what do you say, Sarah?"

"What?" she gasped.

Ten more seconds he waited. "Will you marry me?"

"Yes…" she said, breathlessly.

"Tomorrow?"

"Yesss…"

"Yes, you'll marry me tomorrow?" His voice broke through the veil of passion as he slid his finger slowly across her button to send her over the top.

"Oh yes! Yes! Yeeessssss!"

She bucked. He placed both hands on her hips to keep her seated, thrusting hard for maximum effect. It didn't take long for him to reach his own threshold. His release, long and drawn out, was accompanied by a low growl of absolute pleasure.

He'd never taken his eyes off of her, and now, he waited for it, knowing what to expect once she came to her senses.

"You tricked me."

He smiled at the only woman he'd ever truly loved. "You bet your beautiful ass I did."

"How long have you had that planned?"

"Actually, it just came to me. You always start this conversation, but can't seem to finish it. I don't want to leave anything else to chance, Sarah. I want you to be my wife. I want to get the adoption process started for the girls. I want Danni and Sammi growing up with *my* last name. I want to start our life as a family, now. You said yes…several times...and I'm holding you to every one of them." He threw his head back and gave her his impersonation of her orgasm. "Oh yes! Yess..ss! Yeeessss…"

Sarah punched him playfully in the chest. "Jerk…that is so not what I sound like!" Her laughter rang out in the room as she checked her watch. "Okay, that took all of fifteen minutes. What are we going to do with the next two hours and forty-five minutes?"

He shook his head. "I'm not letting you off the hook. Will you marry me tomorrow?"

She settled back on the pillows. "What are we talking about? You and me at the Lake Coburn courthouse?"

"I don't care what we do, but I know my mother. If she has too much time with you, she'll talk you into some elaborate impersonal gathering with three to five hundred people attending. I'm sticking to *tomorrow*."

Sarah reached over to grab her smartphone and within minutes had verified that they had everything needed for a quickie wedding. "Do you know a judge who can waive the seventy-two hour waiting period?"

"I do. I, along with the grace of God, removed a tumor from his wife's brain. I'll take care of it right now."

"And I'll call Leah."

By the time they ended their calls, plans for an evening wedding at Red and Tiffany's ranch were well underway.

Tanner stared at Sarah, anticipating the moment he could call her his wife. "Can they handle something like that on such short notice?"

She raised her hands. "Babe, I had both Tiffany and Leah on the line and their last words were, 'Don't worry about a thing on this end.' Tiff even told me where to go for a dress, so it looks like a trip to the Galleria is in order, anyway. She said to tell you to wear a tux, and that just because it's a quickie wedding doesn't mean it can't be elegant."

"The Galleria? Today?" He pulled her closer, hoping to get in at least another hour or so of fun before having to leave. Just the thought of it had him rigid again.

Her eyes widened as his hardness brushed against her thigh. "Again?"

"Yep, once more. Then I'll take you shopping and you can buy any dress you want." He flipped her over, settling himself between her thighs. "I cannot wait to call you my wife." He smiled when he pushed into her softness.

Her eyelids drifted shut and she gave a little gasp of pleasure. "I can't wait to be your wife."

He stared down at the miracle of a woman whose love gave him such a profound feeling of satisfaction...of joy. Seeing her smile warmed him through and through. Seeing her smile because of something he did, made his life worth living. Her eyelids opened slowly before giving him what he craved...That smile.

"What's wrong?" Her brow furrowed, one tiny little wrinkle to let him know she was concerned.

He reached up to smooth it away. "Nothing is wrong, Babe. Everything is perfectly right. Now smile for me, Sarah...Smile..."

I hope you enjoyed Sarah and Tanner's story. Please consider leaving a review with Goodreads and/or your favorite book retailer. All reviews, good or bad, are considered constructive.

Thank you so much ~ Lori Leger

MEAGAN'S MARINE (Excerpt)

By
Lori Leger

Chapter 1

"Well, I'll be damned!"

Master Sergeant Mitchell Hebert threw his cell phone on the cot and dropped beside it with a pensive sigh.

Sergeant Matthew "Tex" Broussard swaggered over to Mitch. "You're already in Afghanistan, the arm pit of the middle east. How much more damned could you be?" The east Texas drawl that prompted his nickname in boot camp twenty years earlier, still present and accounted for. "What's up, Cajun Heat?"

"Looks like I'll have time for that barbeque at your place after all, Tex. My only sibling is getting married in a week and my soon to be brother-in-law called to see if I could walk her down the aisle in my dress blues next Saturday. He doesn't want her to know he called me. Wants me to show up just in time for the wedding." He grinned at his friend, his Marine brother he considered as close as blood. "That means I'll be able to make that homecoming celebration of yours in Beaumont Friday afternoon."

Tex beamed at him, revealing his pearly whites. "That's great, man. She still doesn't know you're going home for good?"

"Nope. I want to surprise her. She's been wanting this for so long."

"She'll be surprised all right," Tex snorted. "You're gonna give that poor girl a heart attack on her wedding day. So, what gives with the guy she's hitching? You think he'll be good to her?"

"I think this one's worthy of her, Tex."

"Well, if he ain't, I'm sure you'll be there to whip him into shape."

Mitch stretched out on the cot. "You got that right. I dropped the ball for years with that first son of a bitch she married. That ain't happening again."

"Man, you couldn't stop what you didn't know about. She kept all that from you."

"I know. She took beatings so I wouldn't be distracted over here." He muttered a mild curse. "I owe her, man. She had to deal with my mom's cancer, then dad dying, and she did it all on her own. She was just a kid when I joined up, and she's had it rough."

Tex grunted in agreement before tossing a dirty sock at Mitch. "Well, if that dude's really a brain surgeon like you said he is, she won't have it rough anymore. Big brother will be around this time to make sure nobody's mistreating his little sis. I can understand how you feel, though. God help the poor bastard who *ever* lays a hand on my little sister, Haley."

"Damn straight." Mitch shuddered at the stinky sock and threw it at Tex's back as he left the room. He settled back on his cot and thought about his sister and her impending nuptials to Dr. Tanner Collins.

For nearly a year he'd beaten himself up about nearly losing her to an abusive husband. She'd tried hard to escape, had moved into a woman's shelter and began divorce proceedings. The selfish bastard had tracked her down, kidnapped her and her twin babies. After beating the hell out of Sarah, he'd left her and the girls locked up with no food for nearly a week while he went to work on a land rig. Her breast-feeding had sustained the infants, but had nearly killed their mother. Finally someone had heard the cries and they'd been rescued.

Mitch clenched his fist, regretting his no good brother-in-law had met an untimely demise in the treacherous storm waters of the Gulf of Mexico. What a waste. He'd longed to give the bastard a painful reminder of what a jarhead could and would do to protect his family.

He settled in for an unaccustomed nap, on what would be his last afternoon in Afghanistan. He owed it to his sister and nieces to be *there* for them. Maybe after twenty years as a Marine, he owed it to himself as well.

His eyes drifted shut, and his thoughts shifted from his sister, to a pair of cobalt blue eyes surrounded by long, black lashes. A face materialized suddenly, one with a perky nose, slightly cleft chin, and high cheekbones, framed with hair as black as coal. He pictured the engaging smile of a certain bar maid in Lake Coburn, Louisiana—her straight, white teeth and pouty red lips—lips made for kissing, though he hadn't had the opportunity on their one and only date his last visit home. Not one that counted, anyway.

The initial image faded, turning instead to one of her, this time holding a little boy...the spitting image of his mama. His gut wrenched painfully. No way in hell was he ready for the commitment of a woman with a child.

He winced as Tex's drawl floated to him from outside the tent. Why, he asked himself, for the thousandth time, did Meagan have to speak with the same twang as a guy he saw and heard nearly every day since he'd been back here? Each time he heard it, he couldn't help but think of her.

Mitch folded his pillow over his head, issuing a silent plea that Tex would just once, shut the hell up. It didn't work, of course, as the twang filtered through the barely there pillow.

Meagan.

Not good. Not good at all.

∽

Meagan released her breath in a rush as she entered the room where the bride waited impatiently. "Oh, honey! Tanner is going to flip when he sees you."

Sarah faced the full length mirror, and ran both hands down her sides. "I can't believe it's me in this gorgeous dress." She looked up, catching the reflected gazes of her friends. "It still feels like a dream. No way could I ever be this happy." She smoothed down the delicate layers of champagne colored silk and lace clinging to her slim body. "I just wish my brother could have been here to give me away."

Meagan stepped forward, taking her by the shoulders. "Today's not the day for regrets, Sarah. None whatsoever. You know he'd be here if he could, and he sure as heck wouldn't want you to be sad about it."

Sarah dabbed at the corner of her eye with a tissue. "I know, and you're right, Meg. No regrets. Not today." She spun around, letting the dress flare out around her. "I'm so ready to marry Tanner. Is it almost time?"

A swift rapping on the door had them all pivoting in that direction.

"Is it safe to come in?" Daniel LeBlanc asked, his voice muffled through the thickness of the wooden door.

Tiffany headed to the door and opened it a crack for her father. "As long as you don't have Tanner with you. I don't want him seeing his bride until she's walking down that aisle."

Daniel chuckled, tugging on his elegant black tux. "No, but someone almost as important to her. It seems I'm being robbed of my bride escorting duties for the day."

Tiffany released a shocked gasp a second before opening the door wide enough for the U.S. Marine to enter the room.

Sarah flew to Mitchell and threw her arms around him. "What are you *doing* here, big brother?"

Mitch wrapped his sister in a bear hug. "You didn't think I'd miss your wedding, did you?"

Sarah laughed, straightening her dress as he finally released her. "I didn't think they'd give you leave again this soon. How did you manage this?"

He shrugged a sharply jacketed shoulder. "Turns out your timing was impeccable. I'm out, Sis. For good, this time."

Sarah waved her hands in front of her eyes, trying not to cry. "Seriously? I don't want to ruin my make up, but this would be so worth it."

Even through Sarah's tears and squeals of excitement, all Meagan could do was stare at the vision before her. Mitch Hebert in plain old jeans and a tee shirt was a pleasure to behold. The sight of Master Sergeant Hebert in full dress alpha mode, complete with cover and white gloved, was enough to turn her insides to liquid heat.

Out for good. Permanently. No more praying for his safe-keeping while he was in Afghanistan, *without* his knowledge, of course. *Maybe now she could manage to relax a little?*

A second later, his gaze found hers, pinning her to the spot.

Meagan's breath hitched in her throat at the perceptible widening of his eyes. *Maybe not.*

Red cleared his throat and spoke, breaking her out of her trance.

"Time to get this thing rolling, people. Father Thibodeaux has another wedding in two hours."

Meg managed to slip out of the room without a word to anyone, and made her way to the pew reserved for wedding participants. Although Sarah only had one bridesmaid, Melanie Finley, she'd thoughtfully included her other friends for readings, gift-bearers during the communion for mass, or as witnesses. She'd chosen Meg as a reader for her favorite reading from Corinthians.

Meagan stood with everyone else in the church as Melanie and Red McAllister appeared, each carrying one of Sarah's twin daughters. Groans of admiration rippled through the guests at the sight of the toddlers. The girls were adorable, dressed in matching pink gowns, pristine white shoes, with their glossy curls framed in delicate flower braids. Appreciative gasps turned to laughter, as Sammi and Danni shrieked with delight upon catching sight of Leah and Daniel LeBlanc, seated in the first pew. For all intents and purposes, the couple filled in as welcome replacements for Sarah's deceased parents, and the twins adored them. After all, the LeBlancs were the only grandparent figures they'd ever known.

The bridal march began and all eyes turned to where Sarah and her brother began their leisurely walk up the aisle.

Meagan tried, honestly she did, to direct all her attention on Sarah, the beautiful and glowing bride. She must have given up at some point, because her gaze zeroed in on Mitchell. Sarah's escort carried himself straight and tall beside his sister. Already agonizingly handsome, his uniform gave him an air of masculine elegance that called forth heroes from decades gone by.

She hadn't even realized her mouth had fallen open until his soft brown eyes found hers, rooting her to her spot. She blinked, and closed her mouth in order to swallow a groan of appreciation at the sight of him.

Watching their approach—close—closer still. Close enough to notice a scar at his left temple, just missing his eye. Had that been there before? She didn't think so. What horrors had he seen during his latest months of deployment? What horrors had he survived in his twenty years in the Marines?

Survived. A cold sweat overcame her at the thought. She'd spent lots of time tracking down Christopher's brothers in arms, hoping to find someone who could fill her in on the last days of his life. Her folks hadn't understood her need to know, but at the time, it had been important to her. In the end, she'd heard more than she should have heard, seen more than she should have seen. Everyone else injured in the same incident had survived, in one form or another. Some without limbs, but with enough strength of character to bear their losses well. Others, some with more severe injuries, some with less, hadn't coped so well. Those were the ones who had called *her* dead Marine the lucky one.

During the months that followed her fiancé's death, pregnant with his child, heartbroken and alone, she'd even found herself occasionally agreeing with them. Then came the birth of their son, Buck. She pictured her handsome little boy, with his mother's dark hair, and blue eyes. That's where her traits ended, though. Once she'd set eyes on him, she knew Chris hadn't left her completely. He was there, in the shape of his son's head, to his ears, chin and adorable little nose. He was Christopher made over, and he'd been *her* reason to battle her way out of the darkness.

All too soon, it was time for Meagan's reading. She approached the alter on shaky legs, suddenly terrified at having to read in front of the church full of people. She took a deep breath and tried to relax her shoulders. What was *she*, an unwed mother, doing up here in a church, about to read from the holy bible? Where was that archangel—the one on the lightning bolt committee? Any second now, he'd throw a bolt in her direction, just for being here.

Heat infused her face through and through, accompanied by a feeling of complete unworthiness. She managed to look up, intent on finding an escape route, but instead found Mitchell. He sent her a nod of encouragement from his seat directly in front of the reader's lectern. For some reason, it helped to know he was there. She took a deep breath and found her passage.

"Love is patient. Love is kind. It does not envy, it does not boast, it is not proud..." She continued, making a conscious effort to read slowly, steadily, with full range of voice and inflection, and finally reached the end. *"And now these three remain: Faith, Hope, and Love; and the greatest of these is love."*

∿

Read Cathryn & Zachary's four-part love story first . . .

Then meet Zach's dad, John Michael. Sexy is as much a part of his DNA as those Ferguson-blue eyes.

FULL CIRCLE LOVE

LORI LEGER

RUNNING Out Of *Rain*

Eventually, all storms break for a little sunshine...

PRIME OF LOVE: Book One

LORI LEGER

Sometimes you need to lose all hope in order to find true strength...

HANGING On To *Hope*

"Hanging On To Hope" is her milestone written everywhere. It goes down like a full-bodied wine and a glass overflowing with faith to remind on the second time round can be better than the first."
Bestselling author, Natasza Waters

PRIME OF LOVE: Book Two

LORI LEGER

ABOUT THE AUTHOR

Photo of Ms. Leger provided by Joan Granger of
Simple Memories Photography in Welsh, LA

Lori Leger is a wife, mother, doting grandmother, and
Mistress of Procrastination. She lives in Louisiana with the
love of her life, her very own Studley-do-Right. He's
earned his spot in the Keeper Husband's Hall of Fame by
allowing her to walk away from an eighteen plus year
career as an Engineering Technician in Road Design to
stay home and write.

She adores writing stories set in her beloved
southwest Louisiana, where good Cajun cooking, helping
your neighbors, and saying y'all is as normal as hurricanes,
heat, and humidity. She figures as long as she's not
tunneling through ten feet of snow to get to her car, it's a
perfectly acceptable trade-off.

Lori has ten full-length novels, and one novella
published in three series: La Fleur de Love, its spin-off,
Halos & Horns, and her latest, the Prime of Love series.
She has also contributed to, as well as published, short
stories in each of the five Seasons of Love anthologies, an
author collaboration series. She's compiled four of the
short stories about one particular couple, Cathryn and

Zachary, into a single book called Full Circle Love. It acts as a prequel to the Prime of Love series.

She's contributed to the Sweet & Savory Cookbook of Amazon Authors, published by Top Ten Press. Lori also has an article published in the non-fiction book Writing After Retirement: Tips From Retired Writers, published by Rowman and Littlefield Publishers, and edited and compiled by Carol Smallwood and Christine Redman-Waldeyer.

Hanging On To Hope is the Second book in her Prime of Love Series, novels dedicated to mature characters finding love and laughter through the everyday twists and turns of growing older. She has a third planned for the spring of 2016.

www.CajunflairPublishing.com
www.lorilegerauthor.com
cajunflair@lorilegerauthor.com
lleger641@yahoo.com

Join me on Facebook, Twitter, Goodreads and Pinterest.

www.ingramcontent.com/pod-product-compliance
Lightning Source LLC
Chambersburg PA
CBHW060929120626
46557CB00003B/922